"What sort of compromising positions?"

Mason asked as he slid his hands around her waist and pressed Claire's hips against him.

Her voice grew breathy as she got into their sexy play. "Like, maybe I need to give you something to get that private-investigator role I want so desperately."

Mason watched as Claire licked her lips, slid her hands up his chest and around his shoulders then took one of the buttons of his shirt into her mouth. Before he could stop her, she'd bitten it off and was going for a second one.

"Don't you know how to unbutton a shirt?" he said, though he could hardly give a damn if she cut his shirt off with a machete, so long as they got down to business.

"Sorry, I was just trying to demonstrate my acting skills. Guess I got a little carried away."

"I'm looking forward to your performance."

Dear Reader,

As Hot As It Gets tells the story of Claire and Mason, two
characters from my first novel, *Some Like It Sizzling*. Many
people who read my first novel wrote to me, asking if I was
going to tell this secondary couple's story, and although I hadn't
exactly planned on it, I decided that those readers were
right—Claire and Mason deserved their own book!

I had a blast revisiting these two strong, sexy characters
and discovering how they would find their incendiary path
to happiness. I hope you enjoy *As Hot As It Gets* as much
as I loved writing it. If you'd like to drop me a note and let me
know what you think of it or any of my books, you can reach
me at jamie@jamiesobrato.com, or visit my Web site,
www.jamiesobrato.com, to find out more about me
and my next release.

Sincerely,

Jamie Sobrato

Books by Jamie Sobrato

HARLEQUIN BLAZE

HARLEQUIN TEMPTATION

Don't miss any of our special offers. Write to us at the
following address for information on our newest releases.

Harlequin Reader Service
U.S.: 3010 Walden Ave., P.O. Box 1325, Buffalo, NY 14269
Canadian: P.O. Box 609, Fort Erie, Ont. L2A 5X3

AS HOT AS IT GETS

Jamie Sobrato

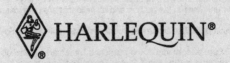

HARLEQUIN®

TORONTO • NEW YORK • LONDON
AMSTERDAM • PARIS • SYDNEY • HAMBURG
STOCKHOLM • ATHENS • TOKYO • MILAN • MADRID
PRAGUE • WARSAW • BUDAPEST • AUCKLAND

To Rich, for showing me how hot it can get

ISBN 0-373-79171-2

AS HOT AS IT GETS

This edition published by arrangement with Harlequin Books S.A.

® and TM are trademarks of the publisher. Trademarks indicated with ® are registered in the United States Patent and Trademark Office, the Canadian Trade Marks Office and in other countries.

www.eHarlequin.com

Printed in U.S.A.

1

ESCAPADE.
Where adults come to play.

Claire Elliot reread the resort brochure some-one had left on her desk. *The creators of the Fantasy Ranch bring you a tropical paradise on a private Caribbean island, an adult playground with every amenity, a hedonistic escape from harsh reality.*

Come. Adventure awaits.

Claire frowned and clicked her French-manicured nails together. Her stomach formed a familiar knot, and she began to suspect that none other than her best friend and co-worker Lucy Walker had been the one to place the glossy magazine-size brochure promi-nently on the top of her in-box stack. In the midst of a slow afternoon at the travel agency, when the Au-gust Phoenix heat was keeping everyone indoors, it was impossible not to be drawn to the images of clear turquoise water, white sand beaches and palm trees casting shade over cool white buildings.

Claire had already heard about Escapade, of

course. It was her job as the manager of Sunny Horizons Travel to keep up with the latest tourism industry news, and word of Mason Walker opening a new adults-only resort had spread like wildfire. She'd had clients calling months ago to book vacations there, many of them fans of Mason's other resort.

The Fantasy Ranch inevitably brought back memories she'd tried hard to forget, memories that haunted her at night when she lay in bed alone. Correction, make that memories of a certain *man* that haunted her on those long sleepless nights.

Mason Walker. The last man she wanted to think about. He was also Lucy's brother-in-law, and her friend had employed some pretty sneaky tactics trying to get Claire and Mason together.

Claire looked up from the brochure and spotted the person she was sure had planted it. Lucy was sitting at her desk trying hard not to look guilty, but she made the fatal mistake of glancing up at Claire's doorway, and the curiosity in her eyes gave her away.

Claire glared at her and crooked a finger in her direction. Lucy rose and came toward Claire's office like a woman condemned. She stepped into the office and closed the door, then flashed Claire a stricken look.

"Before you say anything, just hear me out," Lucy said.

"I thought you'd learned your lesson about matchmaking in Hawaii!" Claire still hated to think about the week she'd spent stranded in paradise with Mason, having been lured there by a fake invitation Lucy had concocted to get the two together.

Not to mention the bachelorette auction dating disaster and the subsequent accusations of a stolen Porsche. Their first encounter at Mason's Arizona resort had left Claire depressed and out of sorts over a man for the first time in the thirty years she'd been alive, and she had no intention of letting it happen again.

Whenever Claire and Mason got together, sparks flew, no doubt about it. But rather than anything sexually incendiary, they were more like the sparks from metal grinding furiously against metal.

"I just thought you should know all about the resort's amenities, that's all. Purely for professional reasons. You wouldn't want to get caught off guard by a client asking you about it, right?"

Lucy was becoming less and less convincing at the Little Miss Innocent act these days.

"And that's the *only* reason you put this on my desk?"

"Absolutely," Lucy said, but her gaze darted out the window over Claire's shoulder.

"You're a terrible liar."

Lucy tried to look offended, but in the end she smiled. "I just think there's something special about the two of you together."

"Yeah, special like an atomic bomb. I don't need

any more explosive relationships." Claire dropped the brochure into the recycling bin next to her desk.

"Aren't you even a little curious about this resort? I mean, *Escapade*—it sounds scandalous. It's billed as being even wilder than the Fantasy Ranch, and from what Mason says, the place is really luxurious."

"What kind of idiot would build yet another resort in the already resort-laden Caribbean?"

"The same guy who turned a failing resort in the middle of the Arizona desert into a smashing success."

"You're a little biased, considering." Considering Lucy had met the love of her life at Mason's Arizona resort. Judd Walker was Mason's younger brother and more than reason enough for Lucy to feel biased with regard to all things Walker.

Lucy smiled. "Maybe a little, but picture what he's done—sultry tropical setting, upscale accommodations, hedonistic atmosphere, a private island…."

"I'll just direct all interested clients to you for information," Claire said in a tone that indicated it was her last comment on the subject.

Lucy's expression fell. "Okay, fine. If that's what you want…"

"It is!" Absolutely. Positively.

But Claire spent the rest of the afternoon feeling distracted and edgy, thoughts of Mason crowding her mind. This was dangerously close to the very same state of misery she swore she wouldn't endure again. She'd been sure she had finally overcome the obsession, yet here she was again, out of sorts at the mere mention of Mason's name.

After leaving the office, Claire navigated the streets of suburban Phoenix in her ragtop Mustang, the top up to protect her from the sun, wishing in the midsummer heat that she could give up her obsession with vintage muscle cars in favor of a nice late-model roadster with reliable air-conditioning.

Instead, she swiped at the perspiration that had formed on her forehead, then rolled down her window. Mirages of water glistened and then disappeared on the sweltering road ahead, and the nauseating scent of car exhaust filled the air.

Either the exhaust fumes were affecting her brain, or the guy in the car next to her bore a resemblance to Mason Walker. Claire blinked and looked at the man again. Definitely not Mason, but close. He had the same dark brown hair, cropped short with a slight wave, the same strong jawline darkened by an uncontrollable five o'clock shadow.

Claire couldn't help but imagine the feel of Mason's rough skin against hers—and actually, imagine was all she *could* do, because they'd never even kissed. On their few explosive encounters, they'd never done anything more intimate than hold hands, and maybe that's why her imagination went into overdrive where Mason was concerned. She'd always gotten her man, so to speak, except for Mason.

And as she sat at a stoplight with the Mason look-alike idling next to her, she felt an unwelcome stirring that started in her belly and radiated down between her legs. Claire sighed and shifted in her seat, but the movement only exacerbated the problem, and she knew what was coming.

The images, fictional as they were, had become all too familiar to her by now. Mason, taking her in a wild frenzy, in some hot, wet, tropical place. She closed her eyes for a moment and didn't notice that the light had turned green until cars behind her began honking their horns. Her eyes shot open and she stepped on the gas too fast, burning rubber as she accelerated through the intersection.

It only made matters worse that Mason's new resort was located in the same kind of lush tropical locale as her fantasies about him. What was that all about, anyway? It was as if he could read her mind, even hundreds of miles away.

Mason had the sort of intense gaze that suggested he might possess such powers, and as she recalled the way his green eyes seemed to see right into her soul, the tension in Claire's belly coiled tighter. The fantasies came at her again, images of his naked body against hers, his tongue teasing her breasts, his hands working unspeakable magic on her.

In this fantasy, like the rest, Claire was powerless to resist him, as helpless and docile as a virgin bride—the exact opposite of her real personality.

She imagined his hard length pressing into her,

filling her with the sweetest sensations she'd ever known....

Then came the impact and the sound of the crash. Her head slammed forward and the seat belt pulled tight against her shoulder as she heard metal crunch against metal and realized she'd just rear-ended the truck in front of her.

She'd managed not to notice the red light, the traffic stopped in the road, the huge semi-truck that her dearly beloved Mustang was now wedged beneath.

Claire blinked at her unnaturally close view of the truck's license plate and felt hot tears forming in her eyes. A moment later when the driver of the semi peered into her window to ask her if she was okay, and she burst into tears, Claire knew without a doubt that something had to give.

MASON WALKER HAD LEARNED the hard way to avoid fiery women. He liked his women compliant, sweet and devoid of any strong opinions. It was easier that way, and it wasn't like he was looking for a serious relationship, anyway. At the age of thirty-six, the bachelor life suited him just fine, and the best way to stay a bachelor was to date the kind of pretty but vacuous women who never seemed to mind that their relationships existed mostly in the bedroom. They were the bonbons of the female persuasion—utterly delicious but nothing to sustain oneself on.

So when he heard Lucy's panicked voice on the

phone asking him if he'd seen Claire Elliot, his stomach dropped to his ankles.

"Why would I have seen Claire?" he asked, already dreading the answer.

He hadn't seen her since that nightmare trip to Hawaii when he'd spent one long, torturous week trying to avoid her, and he didn't ever intend to see her on purpose again.

"She wrecked her car yesterday, and this morning I found a note on my desk telling me that I'm in charge of the travel agency until she comes back—with no mention of where she's gone or when she'll return."

"So?"

"I tried her cell phone, and she has it turned off, but I'm pretty sure she's headed to your island, to Escapade."

Oh, hell.

"Fiery" was only one of a long list of colorful adjectives Mason could use to describe Claire. She was the wildest, most headstrong, infuriating, craziest lunatic of a woman he'd ever met. She was also impossibly sexy—okay, the absolute sexiest woman he'd ever met, too, but that was only until she opened her mouth to spew one of her many strongly held and wrong-headed opinions.

"Why do you think she'd be coming here?"

"Because I, um, sort of talked to her about the resort yesterday afternoon, right before she wrecked her car," Lucy admitted.

The memory of Claire stealing his Porsche and leaving him stranded in the desert came to Mason then. He'd been forced to hitch a ride back to the Fantasy Ranch in the middle of the night—no easy task. And to think that the redheaded bundle of trouble was headed for Escapade at that very moment—

"Lucy, you weren't trying to play matchmaker again, were you?"

"No!" she said a little too quickly. "Well, maybe, but I had no idea she'd just take off like this. I thought she'd need a little more persuading."

It did seem odd that Claire would come running in his direction. After all, she'd been just as adamant about avoiding him as he had been about her.

"Why would she come here? She couldn't possibly want to see me."

Lucy expelled a ragged sigh into the phone. "I'm not sure, but I think it might have something to do with getting you out of her system."

Mason blinked. "What's that supposed to mean?"

"I think Claire is possibly a bit…bothered by the way you two left things."

"Bothered?"

"Or not. Never mind. I shouldn't have said anything."

"That woman is incapable of having a normal relationship with a man."

"Don't be so sure about that," Lucy said.

Mason had to give Lucy credit, she was a smart

woman, and Claire was her best friend—maybe she did know what she was talking about.

"I thought Claire hated me." The lamp she'd clubbed him on the head with in Hawaii had made that pretty clear.

"I don't think it's you so much as it is her inability to control you that she hates."

And that was exactly why he and Claire were never going to happen. She expected men to grovel at her feet, and Mason was not a groveling kind of guy.

"So should I call the police if I see her?" he asked, only half joking.

"No! Just try to forgive and forget."

"Right. Why don't I hand her the keys to my car while I'm at it."

Lucy produced a strained laugh. "Let's don't get carried away. Could you leave a message at the front desk for her to call me as soon as she gets there?"

"No problem—*if* she comes here." Maybe, if he was lucky, she was on her way to Aruba. Or better yet, Siberia. "Is that little brother of mine treating you right?"

"Of course he is. I occasionally have to pry his attention away from the case he's been working too hard on, but I have my methods."

Mason could hear the smile in her voice. In his weaker moments, he felt a tiny bit envious of what his brother and sister-in-law had. But those moments didn't last long because he always remembered how much he hated being tied down, how much simpler the bachelor life was.

After they'd said their goodbyes, Mason hung up the phone and stared at his office door with trepidation. What if Claire was lurking on the other side?

Now wait a minute. Was he really going to let her presence intimidate him? Hell, no. He just dreaded the uproar she always caused, but hey, he owned the resort. If she caused any trouble, he'd have her removed, simple as that.

He expelled a pent-up breath and strode out of his private office into the administrative center of Escapade. The concept for the resort had been brewing in his mind for years, and to see it finally a bustling reality gave him no small sense of satisfaction.

While the Fantasy Ranch, his first venture, was a success, it hadn't been his dream resort. The ranch setting had already existed when he'd taken over the failing business and turned it around. Profits from it had given him the capital to build his second adults-only resort from scratch, exactly the way he wanted it.

The tropical setting, the hedonistic atmosphere, the lush, well-appointed resort—they all combined to make people set aside their inhibitions, let their hair down and have a good time while they were at Escapade. Mason was determined to make this business a success, too, and if their grand opening weekend two months ago had been any indicator, he was well on his way.

He passed through the administrative area and made his way to the reception desk, where he caught his breath at the sight of a woman in the lobby with flaming red hair. Only when he realized it wasn't Claire did he breathe easy again.

"Hi, Mr. Walker," the desk clerk greeted him.

"I need to leave a message for a guest who may be arriving today. Can you check the reservation system to see if Claire Elliot has booked a room?"

The desk clerk checked the computer, then nodded. "She's scheduled to arrive this afternoon, actually. What's your message for her?"

Tension began to build in his temples, and he willed himself to relax again. Mason relayed Lucy's message, then stalked across the lobby to the entryway.

"Mason," a man's voice called from behind him.

He turned to see Carter Cayhill, his friend as well as the resort's entertainment director, striding toward him.

"Hey, Carter."

"You look angrier than those storm clouds outside."

Mason shook his head. "It's nothing. What's up?"

"I just wanted to let you know I may cancel the beach party tonight or move it to an indoor location, depending on when the storm hits."

"Okay, you going to work out tonight?"

Carter glanced at his watch. "I doubt it. Too much stuff left to do."

"I'll catch you later then." They lifted weights together at the gym most nights, but Mason wasn't much in the mood for talking, so it was probably best if he worked out alone tonight.

Carter took off out the door. Outside, palm trees strained against a merciless wind, and the sky had taken on an angry, bruised look. A tropical storm was raging to the southeast, and weather reports yesterday had warned of it turning into a hurricane before it hit the islands.

Definitely not good for business, but Mason wasn't going to let a little foul weather get him down. After all, a hurricane was nothing compared to Claire Elliot blowing into town.

In the distance, a propeller plane was descending toward the island, where it would land on the airstrip Mason had had built for arriving guests. The pressure in his temples became a full-blown headache at the thought that Claire might be on that very plane, that his calm, idyllic existence on the island might soon be spinning out of control thanks to one uncontrollable female.

He headed back to his office, determined to banish Claire from his thoughts. But he couldn't concentrate on work. He sat at his desk, staring at the resort's budget and seeing numbers that made no sense. He tapped his pen on the desk, then decided to try reading e-mail.

He opened his e-mail program and watched as thirty messages downloaded, adding to the hundred or so already waiting in his in-box to be read. He scanned the list of messages, hoping to see a personal one amid the mass of work-related mail, and he was happy to find a message from his brother near the bottom of the list.

Judd had been busy lately with his new marriage and his private investigation business, but he still managed to write or call regularly. His messages were usually brief, but it comforted Mason to know his little brother was out there in the world, doing his thing and getting by just fine. There'd been a time when he'd worried about Judd, but now that Lucy was on the scene, he knew his brother was in good hands.

He opened the message and read Judd's account of his and Lucy's recent weekend getaway to Sedona. The message closed with the usual "what's going on with you" question, and Mason sat staring at it, feeling a vague sense of discontent.

He should have been thrilled for his brother's life, and he was. Pretty much. But he also felt a little thrown off balance by the fact that Judd was a married guy, and every one of his messages underlined that difference between them in some way. It wasn't like Judd did it on purpose. Being married was just a dominant fact of his life.

A small part of Mason missed the years when they'd had bachelorhood in common. Every time one of his friends—and now his brother—got married, it meant there was one more guy on the other side of the fence, and one less running free in the pasture.

Mason had found himself wishing lately that he and Judd lived closer so that they could play basketball together, hang out, do guy things—and so that he could just shoot the breeze with him. But whatever. They could talk on the phone, at least, though it wasn't the same.

What would he have told Judd if he were here, anyway? That he was beginning to resent that so few of his friends were still single? That his normal passion for beautiful women seemed to have waned recently, leaving him alone more nights than he would have preferred? That he was beginning to understand women were more interested in the size of his private island than they were in him as a man?

It struck him then that yeah, he did sort of wish he could tell his brother those things in person. He rolled his eyes at the smarmy turn his thoughts had taken and closed the e-mail program, then stood up from his desk, grabbed his laptop case and headed for the door. He'd definitely let stress affect him, and it was time to head for the gym. Feeling sorry for himself was nothing a good workout couldn't cure.

An hour and a half later, he was in his private suite, feeling invigorated and free of the headache he'd developed earlier. He'd just gotten out of the shower, and if he could figure out where the hell housekeeping had put his clean laundry, he'd be able to get dressed and relax in front of the TV with a beer.

Mason had designed his own space at the resort, where he could oversee business and still escape from harsh reality when he needed to. He tried to keep its location private, so he was surprised to hear a knock at the door as he was peering into the closet, still unenlightened about the whereabouts of his clothes. It was five-thirty, and he hadn't ordered room service, nor had he invited anyone to stop by.

He went to the door and looked through the peephole. The redhead he saw on the other side caused his headache to return instantly. His sense of relaxation evaporated and his body took on the tense, ready-to-pounce feeling he'd come to associate with Claire's presence.

He glanced away, muttered a curse, and looked through the peephole again to make sure he wasn't hallucinating.

God help him, she was here.

She would have had her ways of finding out where he stayed, of course. Claire's hair was tousled from the storm outside, a riotous mess of waves that tumbled over her shoulders. Damp strands clung to her face around her baby-doll blue eyes, reminding him in a flash of the first time he'd known he wanted Claire, when he'd seen her dancing onstage in a wet lingerie contest at the Fantasy Ranch.

She looked just as irresistible tonight, but now he

knew what a pain in the ass she was. He contemplated not answering the door, but his sense of morbid curiosity won out.

After tugging on his work clothes again—not bothering to button the shirt—he opened the door, and Claire flashed him a smile similar to the one Eve must have worn when she offered Adam the apple. Mesmerized by the contrast of her blue eyes and her dark red hair, he was only vaguely aware of her unfastening the belt of her raincoat.

And then she let the front of her raincoat fall open, drawing Mason's gaze downward. She was naked under the coat, except for a pair of black strappy heels.

"I hope you don't mind unannounced visitors," she said.

Mason let his gaze meander from her sexy heels up the length of her thin, shapely legs, pausing at the triangle of hair that made his forehead break out in a cold sweat, then moving up farther, admiring first the delicious plane of her belly, then the silken curves of her breasts. Her pink, puckered nipples gave him an instant erection, and the take-me look she gave him when he finally met her gaze again didn't help matters.

"What the hell are you doing?" he managed to croak.

"Trying to seduce you?"

"Nothing's ever that simple with you." Or that easy.

"I need to get you out of my system, okay? One night, you and me, no strings attached."

Not that he was interested, but Mason couldn't help asking, "No strings attached?"

"No morning after, no follow-up phone calls, nothing. We don't ever have to see each other again. I promise."

Intriguing.

Mason forced himself not to look her over any more, for fear he'd lose all common sense. "What if it doesn't work? What if you do want to see me again?"

"Don't flatter yourself. It *will* work."

Mason smiled. "I've been told I'm addictive."

Claire looked him up and down. "I don't have an addictive personality."

It struck him that this was one of the more civil conversations they'd ever had. So, presumably it just took getting naked to make Claire mind her manners. Mason decided not to explore that thought any further.

"Tempting offer, but you'd better go before I call security."

Claire's jaw dropped, and for the first time since he'd met her, she was speechless.

He almost felt guilty for not inviting her in, but then he reminded himself that this was Claire Elliot, the woman who'd stolen his Porsche and abandoned him in the desert to hitchhike home, and his impending guilt vanished.

"Have a good evening, and I expect you'll be checking out tomorrow," he said, glancing down one last time at her glorious chest, then shut the door in her face.

Mason foresaw the rest of his night then: him, alone in his suite, images of Claire bombarding him, and nothing but a cold shower to keep him company.

2

CLAIRE STARED at the door that had just closed in her face, then remembered from the breeze it created that she was standing there naked with her coat open. She jerked it closed and fumbled to retie the belt at her waist. This door-slamming-in-her-face thing had not been part of the plan.

Her cheeks burned, and Claire knew if she could have looked in the mirror she'd have seen embarrassment and anger splashed across her face, clear as a newspaper headline. She might have been a pretty good actress when she needed to be, but these were two emotions she'd never been able to hide.

She turned away from the door and thanked heaven no one was around. With a few deep breaths and a bit of distance from Mason's suite, she felt relatively calm again.

Of course Mason wasn't going to welcome her with open arms, not after the way they'd left things in Hawaii, and in Arizona before that. She'd been an idiot to show up here naked, thinking her breasts alone would be enough to make Mason forget their differences for a few hours. Which just proved how addled by sexual desire her brain was.

But she would not fail in her mission. No, before she left Escapade, she'd get her man and rid herself of all those unrealistic fantasies—fantasies no man could live up to, let alone a self-obsessed control-freak like Mason Walker.

Yep, once she got him in bed, she was sure her fantasies would be stopped cold by reality. Cold, flaccid, probably-sleeps-with-his-socks-on reality.

Claire smiled to herself as she walked back to her room to come up with a new strategy. The rain had mercifully stopped, though the late-afternoon sky was darkened with storm clouds that looked as if they were going to burst forth with another downpour sometime soon.

Along the way, she couldn't help noting what a great job Mason had done with the new resort. The grounds were lush, landscaped with spiky tropical plants and voluptuous flowers, and filled with meandering pathways that invited long, intimate walks with a lover. The buildings, done in white stucco with Spanish-influenced Caribbean architecture, were pretty and serene, and the quick survey she'd done of her room after arriving earlier had revealed it to be an elegant, well-appointed private retreat.

Escapade was a great concept for a resort, one that catered to hedonistic vacationers who had money to burn. Claire had come there sort of hoping not to like the place, but she grudgingly admitted that Mason was, if nothing else, a very smart businessman.

Halfway across the resort, the rain picked up again, and Claire found herself pelted by fat raindrops. Overhead, the storm clouds were moving fast, and the wind whipped at her hair and threatened to blow her coat open and reveal to the world just how hedonistic she was feeling. But rather than being put off by the inclement weather, the guests she'd seen so far at Escapade seemed to be having a good time regardless. Knowing the laid-back crowd Mason's resorts attracted, she could imagine people coming outdoors for the storm rather than retreating.

In her room, Claire took off the raincoat, dried her hair and dug around in her suitcase for clothes. In her sex-crazed stupor, she'd managed to pack mostly lingerie and nothing suited for curling up in her room alone.

But curling up in her room alone was the last thing Claire felt like doing right now, anyway, so she grabbed her trusty little black dress with the crisscrossing spaghetti straps and tugged it on without bothering to put on a bra. She slipped into a pair of panties and decided to head for the bar she'd spotted earlier. From there, she'd think about finding some dinner. After Mason's rejection of her offer, she needed a little distraction to get herself thinking creatively about how to solve her problem.

She opened the door to her room and was stopped in her tracks by none other than the control-freak himself, standing in the doorway with his hand poised to knock. His physical appearance always made her catch her breath, and now was no exception.

With his dark good looks, his sensual green eyes and his made-for-pleasure body, it was easy to see why she'd been driven to unrealistic fantasies about him. When he kept his mouth shut, he was a total hottie.

"Did you change your mind?" she asked, forcing herself to sound like she didn't care one way or the other.

"No, but I thought we should talk."

"Slamming your door in my face isn't exactly the best way to start a conversation."

"Neither is stripping naked."

"I think my method was the friendlier of the two."

"I apologize. Now can I come in?"

Claire had to admit, she was intrigued by this turn of events. "I was just about to go out, but I suppose you can come in for a few minutes."

There—casual as she pleased. She didn't sound like a desperate hormonal female at all.

She stepped aside and Mason entered the room, filling it instantly with his overbearing masculine presence.

"I'm hoping we can call a truce and part ways as friends. I feel bad about the way things have gone between us, if for no other reason than our mutual friendship with Lucy."

Claire thought of their first date—utter disaster—and their subsequent encounters—disasters every one. There was no denying she was partly to blame, especially if it meant she might get Mason into bed at last. "Okay, truce. I don't know if we can be friends, but we can at least be people who don't hurl sharp objects at each other."

He nodded, a smile playing on his lips. "I think I can live with that."

"Nice resort you've got here."

"Thanks. It's great to finally see it up and running."

"Must have been years of work getting this place built."

Mason gave her a pointed look, as if he were fully aware of her buttering him up for ulterior purposes.

"It was worth it," he finally said. "There's a strong market for upscale resorts."

"Exactly."

He ran one hand through his hair and made a move toward the door. "I should be going," he said.

Claire calculated her next move. Clearly he wasn't going to just fall into bed with her, but then again, he might still be persuaded if she found the right enticement.

"Being at a place like this alone—it's a little odd, you know?"

"Lots of singles come here to meet other people."

"But I don't want to meet just anyone."

"I'm sure you have no problem finding men."

Claire closed the distance between them. How far would she have to go to get him into bed tonight? Her stomach fluttered at the thought of having to humiliate herself again, but what was truly more humiliating? Being so distracted by sexual fantasies that she wrecked her car, or taking charge of the situation and doing what a girl had to do to get her way?

Claire would choose getting her way any day, even if a little begging was involved. "Are you really going to leave me in agony like this?"

"What agony?"

"I want you, Mason." She slid one dress strap, then the other, down over her shoulders, until her breasts were revealed. "Please don't make me beg."

If she wasn't mistaken, Claire would have sworn she could see the color rising on his neck.

"Us sleeping together would be a bad idea," he said without much feeling.

"Or maybe it would be the smartest thing you've done in a long time." She took a half step closer, and her breasts were nearly pressed against his chest.

She slid her hand up his arm and behind his neck. "Just kiss me, and then if you still think our sleeping together is a bad idea, you can walk away and I'll never bother you again."

His gaze was locked on her mouth, and she knew she had him. "You're a wicked woman."

"Wicked can be lots of fun," she whispered, right before their lips collided.

Mason felt the satin texture of Claire's lips, and then her tongue, against his, and he knew he was lost. It had been bad enough that he'd allowed himself to come to her room—damned crazy that he was kissing her.

He slipped his hands around her narrow waist and pulled her against him. He wanted to inhale her, devour her. All her wild, high-strung energy was bound up in that one kiss, and Mason felt himself growing weak in the knees for the first time he could remember. An ache to have her spread from his groin to his fingertips, until he felt as if he were literally throbbing.

She felt better than he'd imagined, and as she clung to him and explored with her tongue, he realized just how much imagining he'd been doing. Claire had been the object of quite a few fantasies since he'd met her, and while he'd always written it off as no big deal, it was.

He wanted her as much as he'd ever wanted any woman—maybe more than he'd ever wanted anyone else, which proved that he had no common sense when it came to romance and no business engaging in serious relationships.

But serious wasn't what Claire wanted. She'd asked for one night only, and that, he could handle, right?

Her hands slid under his shirt, across the bare flesh of his back, and the skin-on-skin contact put his senses on high alert. He hadn't felt so aroused since…since he couldn't remember when. Too bad she made him absolutely crazy every time they tried to get to know each other.

Crazy.

That's exactly what he was if he let this go on for another second. He'd come to Claire's room because he'd been so full of nervous energy he hadn't known what else to do. And he'd truly felt bad about slamming the door in her face. He'd hoped—and still did—that he could send her on her way with no hard feelings. Maybe offer her a free week's stay at the Fantasy Ranch, which would put plenty of distance between himself and Claire.

Distance was desperately needed right now.

Mason summoned all his willpower and broke away from the kiss, then grasped Claire by the shoulders and put her at arm's length. He gently slid each of her dress straps back onto her shoulders, covering her delicious breasts as he did so.

She fired him a glare that could have leveled buildings. "I only came here tonight to prove to myself that you're a lousy lover."

Now there was the Claire he remembered.

"Why would you need to prove that?"

Her glare turned calculating. "There's no denying a certain chemistry between us…."

Yeah, the sort of bad chemistry that left unsuspecting bystanders with third-degree burns.

"Let's just say I have a bit of an overactive fantasy life, and there's no way you can live up to my fantasies."

Mason felt a burst of satisfaction that she'd fantasized about him. "If you're so sure of that, why do you need to prove it to yourself?"

Claire crossed her arms over her chest and expelled a sigh. "My mind and body are not in agreement on the issue."

He had the same damn problem. "Like I said before, it's best if you leave. There's a tropical storm headed this way, and you might be able to fly out tomorrow morning before it hits the island full force."

"If you want me to leave, you'll have to have me physically removed."

Mason thought of Lucy, of how let-down she'd feel if he had her beloved best friend kicked out of Escapade, and he knew he wouldn't be able to do it. Not yet, anyway. Not until Claire gave him a really good reason to use when he had to justify his actions to Lucy.

"I'm sure you'll give me a valid reason to do that soon enough. Until then, try to keep your distance from me, and no more showing up at my door—or anywhere else—trying to seduce me."

Mason turned to the door and opened it, then spun back to Claire to say goodbye. She wore the smug look of a woman who thought she'd won the battle. She was mistaken.

"You're afraid of me, aren't you?" she said.

"No, I'm just smart enough to recognize trouble when I see it."

Mason stepped out into the hallway. As he closed the door, he caught a glimpse of Claire's self-satisfied smile, and for no apparent reason, his sense of victory evaporated into thin air.

MASON WAS PROVING TO BE a harder target than Claire had anticipated, but she wasn't ready to give up. The kiss they'd shared had been more than a little disconcerting because rather than kissing like a dead fish, as she'd hoped he would, Mason's kissing technique was pretty impressive. Maybe even incendiary.

Or maybe she was just so out of her mind with wanting him that she'd become a poor judge of such things.

Yes. That had to be it.

Claire touched up her lipstick in the bathroom mirror, then once again headed for the Cabana Club. This time, she actually made it out into the hallway without interruption. She made her way outside, where the rain still hadn't resumed, but storm clouds continued to hover, and the wind whipped her hair into her face as it caused the plants and palm trees to flail about. She hurried along the path to the public area where she'd spotted the bar earlier, a sense of excitement and possibility filling her.

Maybe she'd see someone at the bar who'd make

her forget all about Mason. Maybe that was the real reason she'd flown all the way here today. She doubted she could settle for one man, anyway, so it was ridiculous that one man dominated all her fantasies. There's no way he could live up.

Claire's standards were too high, her appetite too insatiable, her sense of adventure too strong. Predictability was death, as her father had always said. She blinked away the sudden dampness in her eyes.

Her father, Wilson Elliot, had passed away six months earlier in a car accident, and she still hadn't gotten used to his absence. She'd been Daddy's girl—even if Daddy was usually away on business. He'd always been only a phone call away to offer advice or just a listening ear, and he'd always been there to remind her that no one was good enough for his princess.

Claire forced the melancholy thoughts from her mind when she spotted the glow of the Cabana Club sign. Once inside, she brushed her wind-battered hair out of her face with her fingers. She took a seat at the bar and caught the eye of the bartender, a hunky guy with bulging biceps and a blond buzz cut. He nodded a greeting as he poured a blender drink into a glass, and after he'd served it he made his way over to her.

"What's your pleasure?" he asked with a flirty smile.

"A dry martini." Claire flashed a halfhearted smile at him, hating that she couldn't even muster the energy to flirt back.

When he turned away, she stared hard at his body, to no avail. Damn it, she couldn't even get aroused by such a fine male specimen. And she'd been like this for months. Mason and all the wild fantasies he incited were ruining her sex life, and it had to stop.

A raunchy Prince song was playing over the speaker system. Claire glanced over at the stage and noted that it was vacant. Either the band was on break, or her hopes of watching drunken people dance to Caribbean music were soon to be dashed. Then she spotted a few couples at the edge of the dance floor engaged in the kind of dancing that left little to the imagination regarding what they'd be doing in bed mere hours from now.

What she should have been doing with Mason at that very moment.

How could Mason have turned her down a second time? What, did he have supernatural powers? Maybe he didn't feel the same animal attraction for her that she felt for him. Maybe she was making an even bigger ass of herself than she feared.

"You look like you need this," the bartender said when he returned with her martini.

"I need a lot more than a drink to solve my problems," she said, calculating whether seducing the bartender would be a worthy pursuit.

But try as she might, she just couldn't do more than appreciate him on an aesthetic level. She may as well have tried to leap tall buildings as get her pulse to quicken over any guy lately.

Except, of course, the one she absolutely didn't want to pulse and quake over.

The bartender looked over her shoulder and his expression changed from flirtatious to guarded. "Mr. Casey," he said, all business now, "how can I help you?"

Claire followed his gaze and found a gray-haired man in a white shirt that was open to reveal his hairy chest taking the seat next to hers. She flashed a thin smile at him, hoping he wouldn't take it as a sign to start hitting on her.

He ignored the bartender's question and turned his attention to Claire. "You must be Ashley," he said, placing one hand on her lower back.

Claire shifted her weight away from him, forcing his hand to drop. "No, wrong person."

"Mr. Casey, I believe Ashley's been delayed by a few minutes. Why don't you take a seat over there and have a drink," the bartender said a little too quickly, nodding at the other side of the bar.

His gaze darted nervously toward Claire, and his flirtatious smile was nowhere in sight.

Claire glanced between the two men, trying to guess what exactly was going on as the guy named Mr. Casey moved to the empty bar stool the bartender had indicated. Who was Ashley, and why had the bartender suddenly gotten so uptight? She sipped her martini and watched other people laughing and flirting across the bar. Normally, she would have been one of those carefree souls, but tonight she must have been giving off bad vibes. Bad, Mason Walker-induced vibes.

A few minutes later, a woman Claire guessed was Ashley showed up, clad in a black leather mini-dress that was too slutty even for Claire's taste. After a short conversation with the shirt-button-challenged Mr. Casey, the two left the bar together. Their body language, she noted, was more appropriate for a business deal than a lover's tryst, and her curiosity was piqued.

She eyed the bartender again but doubted he'd offer any enlightenment. And then it occurred to her that he could be in on whatever business dealings, illegal or otherwise, might have been going on between the suspicious pair.

Was the woman a prostitute? A drug dealer? An inappropriately dressed massage therapist?

Without anyone to answer her questions, Claire got bored with the subject and looked around for other people-watching entertainment, but she'd seen it all a million times. Mating rituals performed with the aid of alcohol, loud music and tight clothes. It all just bored her tonight.

Claire downed the rest of her martini. The festive atmosphere in the bar was bumming her out, and the alcohol hadn't helped. What she suddenly wanted more than anything was to be curled up on her couch at home, watching old movies and eating a fudge-brownie sundae. Maybe Mason was right that she should leave before the storm hit, cut her losses, give up on curing her case of Mason-itis.

She pushed herself away from the bar and cast one last glance at the bartender, hoping he might get her loins stirring after all. He caught her eye and smiled, and Claire decided on a whim she'd take a risk and give him her room number. What the heck. If he called or dropped in and they still didn't click, she could tell him to get lost. She found a pen in her bag and wrote her room number on a drink napkin, then turned it around so that the bartender could read it when he came to clear her glass from the bar.

There, now it was in the hands of fate, and she could at least feel like she was being proactive when she went back to her room to sulk. Getting rid of her Mason urges was proving to be a hell of a lot harder than she'd planned.

3

A KNOCK AT THE DOOR interrupted Claire's perusal of the room-service menu.

"What now?" she muttered, pretty sure Mason hadn't returned to grant her wish for a night of mediocre sex.

Then she remembered the drink napkin, and her hopes rose. Could it really be possible that something good would happen to her tonight?

A peek through the peephole answered her question with a resounding "no." Instead of Mason or Hunky Bartender, what she saw was a middle-aged man with a disappearing hairline and an expanded waistline. She'd never seen him before, and he was, coincidentally enough, wearing a raincoat tied at the waist. Claire could only hope he had more clothes on under his than she'd had on under hers.

She considered not answering the door, but curiosity got the best of her. Grabbing a hotel pen from the dresser near the door, she prepared to jab her visitor in the eye if he made any funny moves, then opened the door.

"Yes?" she asked.

"I've been a bad boy," he said, his voice oddly strained. "Are you going to punish me?"

Claire stood there frozen, fully aware that she should be slamming the door at that moment but unable to make her arm move.

When she didn't speak, Bad Boy's expression grew a bit hesitant. "Did I say something wrong?"

"Um…" Where, exactly, should she start explaining everything that was wrong with what he'd said?

"I'm sorry, this is my first time, and, um, maybe you need payment first?" The man started fumbling for what Claire assumed was his wallet, but when he opened the waist of his coat, he revealed that he was wearing a man-size diaper. And nothing else.

Claire emitted a sound something like "eek," and Bad Boy froze, his expression a mixture of confusion and embarrassment.

"Y-you're not the dominatrix, are you?"

The *dominatrix?* An image of the woman in the black leather dress came to mind.

"No, I'm not!"

"But the number I got from the bar was for suite number—"

He withdrew a napkin from his pocket and looked at it, then glanced between Claire and the room number on her door. The sight of her drink napkin caused Claire's stomach to twist into a knot. She was an idiot, and she deserved every bit of this humiliation.

And it was time to get rid of the guy in the diaper. "Wrong room, buddy," she said, then slammed the door before her urge to turn the pen into a weapon became too strong to resist.

She locked the door for good measure, then stood staring at it for what felt like minutes, trying to make sense of the encounter.

Questions whirred through her head. What was going on here? And whatever it was, did Mason know about it?

In the face of such a bizarre crisis, there was only one person to call. Without stopping to question how she'd explain her room number on the drink napkin, she went to the phone and dialed Lucy's number. When her best friend answered, Claire relaxed at the familiar sound of her voice.

"Hi, Luc. It's me."

"Claire! I've been hovering by the phone all afternoon! Why didn't you call me sooner? I was worried sick."

Claire winced at the verbal assault. "Because I didn't feel like listening to you try to talk me out of anything."

"What do I need to be talking you out of? Claire? What are you up to?"

"I just came here to sleep with Mason, that's all."

"That's what I was afraid of! Why didn't you talk to me about this ahead of time? Did you hit your head when you had that accident yesterday?"

"No, my neck's a little stiff, and Daisy's totaled, but I'm fine." Claire felt a pang of sadness over her poor, smashed-up Mustang. That event, more than anything else, had convinced her to do whatever it took to make sure she was a victim to no man's charms, and especially not to Mason's.

"I'm sorry about your car—I mean, Daisy, but don't you think your reaction is a little drastic?"

"I thought you wanted me with Mason."

Lucy sighed into the phone. "I do, but not like this, not as part of some scheme to make yourself forget him."

Claire felt her face burning. Was she really that obvious? Maybe not to the whole world, but to Lucy, who knew her better than anyone, she was. There was no sense in trying to hide anything from her because she always guessed what was really going on.

"You're such a romantic, Luc. Not everyone can have what you and Judd have." Some people, like Claire, just wanted the sense of adventure and possibility that came with being single, and if it meant sacrificing having one true love in order to have her carefree lifestyle, she was pretty sure she could deal with that.

"Of course you can!"

Claire rolled her eyes at the phone. She might as well just accept that Lucy was never going to see eye to eye with her about her lifestyle. Claire loved her job managing the travel agency, loved the opportunities she had to visit exotic places and make love to exotic men, loved never having to deal with the complications that came with long-term boyfriends.

Her life was everything she wanted it to be. Well, almost. Except for her Mason problem.

"We've had this argument already, and there's no point in having it again right now, because Mason has already kicked me out of his suite and told me to leave the resort."

"No!"

"Well, not in so many words, but he got his point across."

"What did you do to him?"

"Nothing much," Claire said, smiling. Lucy would have a conniption fit if she knew the truth.

"Claire..."

"Really! He just wasn't exactly happy to see me, that's all. Understandable, given our history."

"Maybe if you apologized to him—sincerely apologized—"

"Don't worry, I have a feeling me hanging out at Mason's resort is going to be the least of his problems after what just happened a few minutes ago." Claire told Lucy what she suspected was going on at Escapade.

"A *what* service?" Lucy asked, her voice instantly rising to a screechy pitch.

Claire held the phone closer to her mouth and over-enunciated, "A *dom-in-a-trix* service. Do you think Mason is capable of being involved in something like that?"

"Absolutely not. No way. He'd never—"

"Okay, okay. I thought that's what you'd say, but I wanted to be sure."

"Are you sure it's really a—a dominatrix service? I mean, how do you know?"

Claire explained the incident at the bar followed by the one at her door. "I'm not totally sure, but I'd be willing to bet that's exactly what's going on," she said, happy that she'd managed to tell the story while carefully avoiding any mention of the drink napkin. She couldn't quite explain how that mix-up had occurred, anyway. It just would have muddied the water.

"Mason's going to be furious. This could ruin the reputation of his business if word gets out."

"Yeah," Claire said, not exactly feeling sorry for Mason, but surprisingly not gleeful either. "He's going to have to crack down on it right away and try to keep the news of it quiet…. Or who knows, maybe wild rumors about the place are just what he needs to keep business booming."

"That's not Mason's intention. He wants Escapade to be more about luxury and less about sex. He's not going to like this one bit—you've got to tell him right away."

"Why should I help him? He wouldn't help me if my life depended on it."

"You're not giving him enough credit, and you

should help him because it's the right thing to do. And because it might mend a few fences between you two."

"I don't want any mended fences—I just want him to sleep with me."

"You can't have one without the other," Lucy said.

"Believe me, I don't have to like him to sleep with him, and vice versa. In fact, it's impossible for me to like such an arrogant, pigheaded—"

"You're talking about my brother-in-law. I don't want to hear it."

Claire rolled her eyes at the phone. "Okay, fine. I see where your loyalty lies."

"Stop pouting—you know I want what's best for you."

Okay, so maybe she did, but that didn't mean she had any idea what really was best for Claire. Lucy thought Claire needed to settle down, get married and do the family thing, but Claire knew she was too restless for such a limited future. She needed freedom, adventure and a different guy for each season, preferably.

But that thought reminded her that she hadn't had a single summer fling yet this year—and not a spring one, either, for that matter. Summer was quickly passing into fall, and she hadn't been able to summon any real interest in a guy besides Mason since…last March, at best.

Yikes.

Maybe helping Mason was just what she needed to do to break down his I-hate-you-too-much-to-sleep-with-you barrier, and then she'd be free to fling to her heart's content.

"Luc, I gotta go. I just remembered something I need to do."

"You're going to tell Mason, right?"

"Um, right. Talk to you soon. Bye!" And she hung up before Lucy could issue any dire warnings about what might happen if Claire behaved irresponsibly.

She checked her lipstick in the mirror, fluffed her hair up a bit and readjusted her dress to ensure maximum cleavage. There—now she was armed for seduction again, and she had a new weapon in her arsenal. She smiled to herself as she set off for Mason's room again, determined not to leave this time until she'd gotten her man.

MASON PEERED THROUGH the peephole and muttered a curse under his breath. The redheaded devil was back.

Damn it.

Maybe he just shouldn't answer. Or maybe he should call security now before things got out of control. But curiosity got the best of him again.

"What do you want?" he called through the door.

She looked him in the eye through the peephole and offered a tentative smile. "We need to talk about a problem," she called back.

"The only problem we need to talk about is you leaving before I have to call security."

He spotted the flash of anger in her eyes, which she quickly subdued.

"There's something going on here at Escapade that you need to know about. Do you want to stay in the dark or let me in and listen to what I have to say?"

Mason couldn't tell if she was bluffing, but it was a sure thing that Claire wasn't offering any helpful information about his business. "You expect me to believe you're here to help?"

"Lucy insisted."

That, he could believe. With all his better instincts protesting, he unlocked the door and eased it open. Immediately, his body had its usual animal reaction to Claire.

"What?" he said, trying hard to ignore the sensation of increased blood flow to his guy parts.

"I don't think this is something you'll want discussed in the hallway," she said, eyeing the inside of his suite.

Mason reluctantly stepped aside, half-convinced that she was lying in order to pull some kind of Claire Elliot stunt.

She entered the room and took a seat on the sofa as if she owned the place, then patted the cushion next to her.

"I'll stand," he said, then set the timer on his watch. "You've got five minutes."

Claire raised an eyebrow at him. "So, what do you think of domination and submission?"

"As in S and M?"

"Mmm, hmm. Whips, chains, scary chicks in leather chaps. Does that do it for you?"

"Not especially. What does this have to do with Escapade?" Knowing Claire, this was probably her idea for improving business.

Her smug expression suggested she had a secret she was enjoying a little too much. "Did you know you have a dominatrix-for-hire service operating here at the resort?"

"A *what?*"

"I guess you didn't know then."

"What the hell are you talking about?" Mason felt all the heat dissipating from his groin and relocating to his temples.

"A little while ago a man came to my door with some pretty odd requests, considering I'd never seen him before in my life."

"That's not necessarily unusual here, you know," Mason said, remembering a few incidents of guests getting carried away that his employees had already witnessed.

Mason listened as Claire told him what she'd seen at the bar and then at her door, and the more he listened, the more he got the urge to punch something. Just last year business at his Fantasy Ranch resort had nearly been ruined by a vindictive ex-girlfriend who'd cooked up a sabotage plot to get even with him for dumping her. And now he had scumbags operating a dominatrix service on his new resort? Why did this kind of thing happen to him?

"Somehow I don't think you'd just tell me this out of the goodness of your heart," he said when she finished.

Claire's eyes flashed a spark of pure mischief. "I've got more, and I might even know who's running the show, but I'll need a little incentive to tell you anything else."

Mason reminded himself to breathe. Deep, cleansing breaths. No more angry thoughts.

"You're asking for a bribe?"

"Well, a sort of sensual bribe, I guess you could call it."

"Claire, whatever you're thinking, forget about it," Mason said.

She took a step closer to him, and suddenly the faint dampness of her lips was an offer almost too tempting to refuse. She smiled a luscious, wicked smile. "Make love to me, just for tonight, and I'll tell you whatever you want to know."

Claire slid her hands up his chest, pressed her tight little body against him, and Mason considered resisting. Could he live with himself if he accepted her condition? Would a night with Claire finally get her out of his hair for good?

He wasn't sure he wanted to know the answer.

4

HE STILL FELT NOTHING like a cold fish.

He was all hot flesh and hard muscle, just like in her damn fantasies.

Claire was sure though that she only needed to get Mason into bed to prove that he was anything but fantasy material. One mediocre night—that's all she was asking for.

She tilted her head back, tugged him toward her, and he accepted the offer of a kiss. A long, hot, demanding kiss with a promise of so much more to come. Definitely not the kiss of a cold fish.

Her insides grew warm and tingly, and a spinning-out-of-control sensation overtook her. Nothing mattered except Mason's heat, his touch, his kiss. Even his five o'clock shadow scraping against her face felt good, and she was just about to rid him of his shirt and find out how his bare chest felt beneath her fingertips when he broke the kiss.

"How do I know you're not lying about this extra information?" he asked, a little breathless.

"You don't. Guess you'll have to trust me." Claire realized a moment too late what a risky proposition that would be for him.

She watched doubt form in Mason's eyes, and she felt her chance to score tonight slipping away yet again. She had to do something.

Fast.

"This is crazy."

He took a step back, but Claire tightened her grip on him and steeled herself for more possible humiliation. "Yeah, it is crazy. So do it, anyway, and I'll be gone tomorrow."

"After you give me this mysterious information, right?"

"Of course."

"If it's something you found out, then I can find out on my own, too."

"You don't have time to play detective. You're a busy man, and this is a direct threat to your business."

His doubtful gaze turned calculating, and Claire saw her chance. She shifted her hips so that her body molded to him, and she slid one hand down his chest, the other down his back and over the firm muscles of his ass.

He felt too good to let go of.

Then he gave in.

He wrapped his arms tight around her and devoured her with another kiss. As his tongue caressed hers and his hands burned trails across her backside,

Claire felt herself melting. He still bore an unsettling resemblance to the man of her fantasies, and she was having a hard time being upset about it.

She'd hoped he would at least have doggy breath or an odd body odor—anything to remind her that this was real life. But no, he smelled of soap and something faintly evergreen, and his scent only added to his sex appeal.

Damn it.

A gust of wind whipped through the room, and Claire imagined for a moment that they were creating their own storm. When Mason broke their kiss and looked over his shoulder at the real source of the wind gust, she noticed for the first time that he had a pair of French doors standing open.

Outside she could see a private oasis, a lush garden surrounding a large veranda, with what looked like a hot tub tucked into one corner. Palm fronds and other exotic plants whipped and swayed in the wind, and beyond them, the sky had taken on a foreboding darkness.

Yet all Claire could think about were her tropical fantasies of Mason taking her in some lush, wet place. Drops of rain pelting their naked skin, their own wild animal sounds mingling with the music of the storm….

What better way to nip her most annoying and recurrent fantasy in the bud than to act it out and rid it of its potency?

Yes.

"Let's go out there," she said.

Mason gave her a look she was all too familiar with. "In the storm?"

"It's not really storming yet, just raining a little."

Okay, the occasional bursts of heavy rain were bordering on torrential, but that didn't matter in the face of her determination. This close to the prize, she wouldn't stop running the race.

She was only one boring night away from ridding herself of Mason Walker for good.

He cast a skeptical look outside, then back at her. "I'm not going out there."

"Fine." It didn't have to happen outside. It just had to happen. "If you want to be a pain in the ass about it—"

"If anyone's a pain in the ass, it's you."

"Has anyone ever told you you're overbearing?" Claire said, annoyance throwing a damper on her desire.

"I think you probably have." He silenced her with another kiss, but Claire pulled back.

"That's the kind of thing I'm talking about."

He exhaled a ragged breath. "What? You beg me to have sex with you, and now you don't want to kiss me?"

He made her sound crazy when he said it like that. "That's not what I mean."

"I don't even think you know what you mean. How the hell am *I* supposed to understand you?"

"Are we going to do this or not?"

"In here. Not outside."

"Fine, I wouldn't expect anything interesting from a control freak like you."

"Excuse me? If you think I'm going to be a boring lover, you're wrong."

Claire unzipped her dress and let it fall to the floor. "We'll see about that."

His gaze dropped to her breasts, then her belly, then lower. He took his time studying her from head to toe, probably trying his best to make her feel uncomfortable. He was toying with the wrong woman.

"Your turn," she said.

But he didn't make a move to get undressed. "Fine," he said finally, unbuttoning his shirt.

"Try not to enjoy this too much," she said.

"Believe me, I won't have to try."

Claire's temper flared. She'd never been accused of being a lousy lover, and it occurred to her for the first time that she hadn't quite planned how she'd behave during their encounter. Would she put all of herself into it, try to act like she was enjoying it? Why would she?

This was definitely a problem she'd failed to anticipate.

She'd always taken pride in never faking it with any guy. And now what? Surely she'd have to fake something to get through having sex with Mason....

Except nothing about the burning inside her felt

fake. That much, she could be sure of. Maybe once things really got rolling, she'd have some trouble and have to summon her acting skills to get through the ordeal—or maybe for the first time in her life she'd just have to lie there and bear it.

Maybe, or maybe not.

Mason stalked over to her and grasped her waist, pulled her against him. "You're going to have to stop with the attitude if you want this to work."

"You call this attitude? I thought I was being nice."

"Haven't you ever heard that old gather-more-bees-with-honey saying?"

"Other guys think I'm plenty sweet enough," she said, not exactly sure it was true. She could be fun, wild, interesting…but sweet? It wasn't a word she'd ever heard used to describe her. "Do I actually need any bees? Because I can think of far better uses for honey—"

"You know what I mean."

"You're trying to boss me around again. Can you just not be in control for five minutes?"

"Babe, this is gonna take longer than five minutes."

Claire gave him a once-over. "I'll bet."

This was so much harder than she'd thought it would be, which only illustrated exactly how crazed she'd become.

Mason crossed his arms over his chest, and he said at the same moment as her, "This isn't going to work."

There was an awkward pause.

"Right," Claire said, her temper barely in check. "It's not. I'm leaving."

How many more times could she actually get naked in front of this man without getting laid?

Furious, she snatched up her dress and hurried to put it back on and zip it.

Mason watched her without speaking.

"If you want to know any more about your little dominatrix problem, you can just track the information down yourself. I'm not helping you any more than I already have."

She turned on her heel and headed for the door.

"I can find out whatever I need to know," he said.

Claire opened the door, walked out and slammed it, realizing even as she did so that she'd just flown all the way to the Caribbean for nothing.

MASON GRIMACED at the slamming of his door and stalked across the room, his head swirling with images of Claire standing naked before him. Snippets of conversation played over and over in his mind as he thought of all the things he should have said or done. He hadn't handled the encounter well.

He never handled Claire well, and now he saw the problem. She couldn't be handled or managed or controlled. Not the way he liked, and that was why she drove him to the brink of insanity every time she came near.

But she'd been oh so near, and oh so alive. Hot,

delicious, intoxicating… The way she'd kissed him had left him dizzy with desire, and now he was alone in his big, empty suite. He crossed his arms over his chest and glared out the window at the garden, lit by spotlights. As if his trouble with Claire weren't enough, there was this problem she'd brought to him.

A dominatrix-for-hire service operating on his resort? If it was true, it had to be stopped as soon as possible. The image he wanted for Escapade was hedonistic luxury, and he knew all too well there was a fine line to walk between hedonism and blatant sleaze. It was a battle he'd fought for years with the Fantasy Ranch, and he knew he'd face the same challenge with Escapade. He just hadn't realized how soon the challenge would arise.

Damn it.

He stalked into the bedroom and collapsed on the bed, too frustrated to think straight. Possibilities whirred through his head faster than he could consider their likelihood.

Mason rolled from one side to the other, punched his pillow, then tossed it aside altogether because it felt like a rock beneath his head. But that left him lying on the too-stiff mattress, his body tensed for action and aching for companionship.

Claire Elliot had driven him to distraction.

And he had to have her.

The thought came to him fully formed, as sure as if it were his own name.

But it was ludicrous. She'd just been here, naked and willing, and he'd sent her away. It had been the right thing to do.

Maybe if they could keep their mouths shut long enough to get it on…

He had to have her tonight.

It was time to stop playing musical doorways and get the deed over with, just as she'd proposed. Her idea wasn't nearly as warped as it had sounded at first, and now he was suddenly sure that the only way to get over her was to get in bed with her.

Before he could change his mind again, Mason shot out of bed, then took off for Claire's suite. He made it to the building where she was staying in record time, almost as if the wind from the brewing storm had lifted him and carried him to her.

He knocked on her door, but heard only silence on the other side. After a minute had passed, he knocked again.

Nothing.

Damn it. Where would she have gone, if not back to her room? Claire was a party girl at heart, and it didn't take a genius to figure out that if she wasn't here, she had to be at one of the resort's nightclubs or bars.

But which one? There were three bars and two nightclubs, plus a nightly beach party. Given the weather, he could assume the beach party probably wasn't a happening place right now or had been canceled altogether. He decided to start with the nearest nightclub and headed that way.

Inside Carnivale, the decorating scheme was Brazilian and the music tended to inspire the dirtiest sort of dancing. Mason guessed it was Claire's kind of nightspot. He scanned the dimly lit bar and the crowded dance floor, but didn't see any redheads. Possibly the only convenient thing about Claire was that her fiery red hair made it impossible for her to blend into a crowd.

Mason wandered around the perimeter of the dance floor and was about to give up and head for the next closest club when he caught a telltale glimpse of red from behind a clump of people.

Bingo.

"Hey, Mr. Walker, how's it going?" a waitress asked as she wandered past.

The clump of people moved and he had a clear view of Claire now.

"Fine thanks." He glanced at her name tag. "Diane, could you do me a favor and take a drink to that redhead over there?"

"Sure."

"And a note, too." He kept his gaze on Claire, who was oblivious to his presence as she sat at the bar.

She was sipping a nearly empty martini and scanning the crowd of dancers, bebopping casually to the beat of the music. His entire body was tensed, on alert, as he watched her. A woman who looked like

Claire couldn't spend more than a few minutes alone in a bar before some guy would swoop in.

He had no reason to feel like she was his to claim—he was crazy to feel that way—but he did.

"You want to send her another martini?" the waitress asked.

Mason nodded. "And if you could stop back here on your way to give it to her, I'll have the note ready."

She smiled and gave him a knowing wink, and Mason felt like a fool for no particular reason.

He took a seat at the far end of the bar, where Claire wasn't likely to spot him right away. He requested a pen from the bartender, then grabbed a drink napkin and tried to decide what he would write. One thing he could be sure of was that if he just approached Claire, she'd storm away. He needed to send her a note that would appease her, make amends and lure her outside, where they could talk without an audience.

"I'm sorry," he wrote. "Come back to my suite. Maybe if we just keep our mouths shut and get down to business, we can do what you came here for."

That was about as close to groveling as Mason could get.

The waitress picked up his note, and he watched as she delivered it, along with the drink, to Claire. She read the note, a sexy little frown creasing her brow, then looked up and around the club.

After a few moments, she spotted him. Their

gazes locked, and while he didn't see a blatant invitation in hers, she wasn't running away, either.

He rose from the bar stool and wove his way through the crowd to her. Without saying a word, he pulled her to him and kissed her, long, deep and hot. He put all of himself into that kiss, made it an irresistible promise of pleasures to come.

She felt so right in his arms, it was hard to imagine they'd been ready to strangle each other such a short time ago. And then she grabbed his hand, led him through the crowd onto the dance floor, and started gyrating against him.

Driving him out of his mind.

He had no choice but to dance.

The pulsing beat pounded his head, and Claire's body against him was a stronger force than any intoxicant. The crowd of dancers around them seemed to pulse with the music, their bodies becoming one living mass, and soon Mason didn't notice people bumping against him. He felt only Claire's heat, only her hands grasping his hips, only her gaze pinned on him.

It was too loud to talk, too crowded to escape. They could only dance, and he grew hard against her abdomen. If she'd invited him to make love to her right there on the dance floor, he wasn't sure he'd turn her down.

The music changed from an up-tempo dance number to something distinctly tribal, with a heavy drum beat that seemed to call to his most primal instincts. And the lights in the club changed. They dimmed and then went black, with flashes of light that made visibility possible for brief moments at a time.

Black, white, black, white, black, white… It quickly became clear that trying to focus on seeing was pointless. He simply had to forget everything else and dance. But he got brief glimpses of other dancers, and it seemed that people were becoming more uninhibited the harder it became to see. The longer they danced, the hotter it got on the dance floor, and it seemed as though people were removing items of clothing. He saw flashes of breasts, naked torsos, bodies intertwined in intimate dance moves….

He realized with a start that the couple next to them wasn't just dancing. Flashes of bare hips moving together, pounding against each other, naked body parts exposed, mouths kissing breasts…

They were having sex on the dance floor.

Mason should have told them to get a room. As the owner of the resort, he should have been alerting security or something. But knowing what was going on, having Claire pressed against him, her hands grasping his ass now, her hips moving in time with his, her body a blatant invitation to do exactly what he was aching to do—it was all an incredible turn-on.

And then she did the one thing he was pretty sure would lead to his ruin.

She unzipped his pants and slid her hand inside, grasping his erection. He couldn't wait any longer.

What better way to have sex with Claire than in an environment where they couldn't talk, couldn't be mistaken that this was anything more than a one-night fling?

They were close to the wall, and with a little elbowing, he was able to guide them over against it in the darkness. In the flashes of silvery light, he caught images of Claire, her eyes glazed with arousal, her skin covered in a sheen of sweat, her body moving to the tribal beat.

He lifted her against the wall and she wrapped her legs around him. He pushed aside her panties, slid his fingers inside her, found her even hotter on the inside than she was on the outside.

Out of the corner of his eye, he saw another couple getting it on, the woman bent over the dance floor railing and the man thrusting into her from behind, and he felt electrified. It was a bizarre sensation to realize people around him were having sex, an unexpected and powerful turn-on.

But now that he had Claire against the wall, he realized he needed a condom. He managed to remove his wallet from his pants and find one inside.

"Would you?" he asked Claire, without being sure she could hear him over the music.

She understood. Ripping open the package with her teeth, she made quick work of the task, her gaze riveted on Mason the entire time, as if daring him to really go through with what they were about to do.

He didn't need a dare. He was too far gone to care about anything but easing the ache inside him, driving his cock into Claire until he could regain some sense of control.

She squirmed her hips against him, and then he did it.

He thrust inside her tight opening, all the way inside until their bodies crashed together like ocean and shore.

Any minute now, he'd be okay again. Just a little bit longer, and he'd have his fill of Claire.

But those sensible thoughts were obliterated by the incredible feel of her body, by the sweet tightness that encased him, by the glazed arousal he could see in her eyes, by the intoxicating music, by the tangled bodies he'd seen in the flashes of light.

He thrust into her hard and fast, again and again, unable to slow down. She felt like no woman he'd ever had before, and in the back of his mind, he knew he might be in trouble. Her body felt like the temple where he'd been born to worship, and he imagined that if he could only drive himself deeper inside her, he might find all the answers to all his questions.

Claire pushed down her dress and bared her breasts to him, and he tasted each one, sucking them as if they might quench his suddenly unquenchable thirst.

His hands gripping her ass, holding her tight, as he pumped into her, they moved toward climax faster than he'd expected, both overcome by the sexual turn the night had taken. And then he felt her muscles contracting around his cock, saw in a flash of light her eyes closed and her face transformed with pleasure, and he let himself go, too.

With one last thrust, he came long and hard, spilling into her in wave after wave of pure, white-hot pleasure, an orgasm so intense he nearly collapsed on the dance floor. His body shook as he held her against the wall, aftershocks overtaking him.

Claire's orgasm passed, and she placed a long, deep kiss on his mouth, her tongue eager and inviting.

His heart pounded in his ears, or maybe it was just the music. His body was drenched in sweat, and he was all too aware now that he was in the midst of an orgy, his body still locked together with Claire's.

This was not exactly what he'd planned.

Nor had it been dull or anything near an encounter that would rid him of his desire for Claire. Instead, he wanted to drag her back to his room and spend the rest of the night making up for lost time.

And then he felt a hand on his ass, though Claire's were on his shoulders. A woman wearing only a lace bra and panties danced next to them, her gaze an open invitation.

"Can I join you?" she asked, reaching out and stroking Claire's bare arm.

"No thanks," Mason said.

Claire seemed unfazed by the offer, as far as he could tell, but since most women were either very enthusiastic or very offended by the idea of a ménage à trois, he decided then that they had to get out of the nightclub before all hell broke loose. He might have had his share of multiple-women fantasies, but he knew they were just that—fantasies that had no business being acted out in real life.

He withdrew himself and eased Claire to the ground, then spotted a garbage can at the edge of the dance floor, where he disposed of the condom and arranged himself back in his pants. When he turned back to Claire, intent on leading her out of the club, he wasn't exactly prepared for the sight of her dancing with the woman in the bra and panties.

In the flashes of light, he could see that Claire's dress was back in place, and her arms were raised over her head as she moved to the beat of the music. Claire kept her gaze locked on Mason as the women's bodies pulsed together, performing a dance so erotic his erection came back instantly.

This woman, the hot, infuriating, sexy-as-hell woman…

She crooked a finger at him, inviting him to join the dance. For a moment, he was tempted. Two beautiful women, one hot night…

The woman had her hands on Claire's hips now,

their bodies moving together, their mouths inches apart. She was toying with him, playing some kind of game he hadn't quite guessed yet. Mason's pulse quickened until he felt as if he'd just run a race.

He grabbed Claire's arm and offered the other woman a conciliatory smile, then pulled Claire away before she could protest. Holding on tight to her, his mind racing, his body aching, his every male fiber protesting that he'd just passed up the opportunity for a threesome, he weaved them through the crowd of dancers as fast as he could.

A few minutes later, he'd navigated her out of the nightclub and into the windy, rainy night. A foot-lit path led from the nightclub out in several directions, and Mason chose the most direct route toward his suite. But Claire pulled back, stopping them at a bench among the rustling palm trees.

He turned and looked at her as fat raindrops from the palm fronds pelted them at odd intervals. The wind caused her dress to mold to her body, and her skin was damp with perspiration and rain. Damp tendrils of her wavy hair clung to her face. She looked like the embodiment of sex.

"What the hell was that?" he demanded.

She shrugged, her mouth curving in a coy smile. "Just a little fun. Why'd you drag me out of there so fast?"

"Why were you dancing with that woman?"

"Weren't you tempted?"

"What guy wouldn't be?"

"But you weren't tempted enough to join us." She tugged her hand away from his and crossed her arms over her chest.

"I've got other plans in mind," he said, deliberately letting his gaze drop to peruse her body.

"Oh." Her voice had dropped several octaves. "You're right—once isn't enough."

"No."

"We may need the whole night for my plan to really work."

"You didn't answer my question—why did you start dancing with that woman?"

Claire sighed a put-upon sigh. "Honestly, I've never had sex on a dance floor before, and I've never made out with a girl, either. Guess I thought I'd try to make this a night of firsts."

"Were you trying to get rid of me?" he asked.

"By inviting you to have a ménage à trois? I thought all guys loved them."

Something about her tone was tense and false, and Mason began to get the true picture.

"It would have made it a hell of a lot easier for us to part ways," he said. A pretty sneaky way for her to get rid of him.

She shrugged. "Maybe I was giving you an easy out."

A question formed in his head—was it even possible to have an easy out after what had just happened?

Something so intense, so out of control, so incredible…

"I like my sex one-on-one," he said, wiping rainwater from his brow.

A mischievous look crossed her face. "I do, too."

"Come back to my suite for the night."

Overhead, thunder rumbled and the sound of rain pelting leaves increased. A gust of wind assaulted them, and in a matter of seconds the rain turned into a torrential downpour.

In the half darkness, through the assault of rain, he saw unmistakable arousal darken her gaze.

"We still have more work to do—" She said, raising her voice over the din of the storm.

"Lots and lots of work."

"Right."

Mason took her hand and led her running through the downpour back to his suite, and mercifully, Claire didn't fight, didn't resist, didn't complain.

She was his for the taking.

5

THEY WERE SOAKING WET.

For the first time since she'd arrived on the sultry island, Claire actually felt cold. She was soaked from head to toe, and it had become so difficult walking in her strappy heels that she'd been forced to stop and take them off, going barefoot most of the way to Mason's suite.

Where his hand grasped hers was the only place she felt warm—no, make that hot. His touch nearly seared her, as did the memory of their encounter on the dance floor. Having sex with Mason had been the most intense, uninhibited sex she'd ever had.

She'd been to her share of nightclubs, but she'd never seen an orgy break out, and realizing what was happening had been an incredible turn-on, more so than she ever would have guessed.

And Mason…

Yow.

It had to have been the setting, the wild goings-on, because having sex with Mason on the dance floor had been the most exciting experience of her life—and she'd had some pretty exciting experiences.

But nothing compared to what had just happened.

She'd been so thrown off balance by the encounter, it had only seemed natural to accept the woman in black lace's invitation to dance.

Yes, she'd done it mostly because she'd thought if things went very far and Mason joined in, seeing him making out with another woman would be enough to kill her desire for him. She was having a hard time feeling regretful that her little ploy hadn't worked.

They just needed the rest of the night. Outside of the wild, uninhibited nightclub setting, surely their lovemaking couldn't be as exciting. They could burn off their steam, and with any luck Mason would prove himself to be a bore in bed as she'd always suspected.

The question that kept popping up in her head though was, but what if he wasn't? What if their every encounter was just as hot as the first? What if it was even hotter when they were alone to explore, take their time and find each other's rhythm in bed?

What if having sex with Mason was as hot as it gets, and all her out-of-control fantasies came true?

Mason closed the door of his suite, then turned on a lamp, and Claire forced the nagging questions out of her mind. They were alone, and she ached for him more now than she had before they'd had sex.

They were dripping all over his floor, but he didn't seem to notice.

His gaze was riveted on her as he began removing his wet shirt, then his shoes, socks and pants. Even his boxers were soaked, she noticed, as he peeled them off.

Snapping out of her daze, she tossed her shoes aside and stripped off her dress and panties, their soaked state reminding her of the first time she'd met Mason at the Fantasy Ranch. She'd just won a wet lingerie contest where the audience bid on the winner for charity, and Mason had won an evening with her.

Now he stood before her naked, his erection straining upward—an impressive length longer than the nubbin she'd hoped he would have. His body glistened with rain droplets in the lamplight, looking like some drenched Greek god.

He was just as glorious with his clothes off as he was with them on. And he hadn't even left his socks on.

Damn it.

Claire studied him closer, hoping to see some physical flaw like a third nipple or maybe some fur on his shoulders, but there was nothing out of place. Just a specimen of male physical perfection standing before her.

Mason took one step forward and erased the distance between them. "You're cold," he said, as he slid his hands around her hips. "Maybe we should take a hot shower and get this rainwater off."

"Maybe," she said, too mesmerized by the feel of

him against her to think straight. His erection pressed into her belly, reminding her of how exquisite he'd felt inside her a short time ago.

But she wanted him now. No time for showers, no time for washing and fumbling with awkward shower wall positions—though Mason had proven himself quite adept at doing it up against the wall.

He dipped his head and covered his mouth with hers, explored her with his tongue, slid his hands down to cup her ass, letting his fingertips explore until he'd coaxed the ache inside her into a throbbing need so consuming she could think of nothing else.

"Or maybe later…" she whispered as she pulled him to the floor. Wrapping her legs around his hips, she shifted her own until he was straining at her opening, and nothing stood between her and sweet satisfaction.

"We need protection," he said.

"Oh, right."

"I'll be right back."

Claire lay on the floor, her every nerve ending alive with anticipation, as he disappeared into his bedroom, but it was far too passive a position for her. She believed in going after what she wanted, so she got up and followed him into the darkened room, re-calling his note in the nightclub.

If they could just keep their mouths shut, they'd both get what they wanted and she could be gone tomorrow.

Now the air-conditioning inside the suite was

making her damp skin turn to gooseflesh, and she craved Mason's heat more than ever. Her hair was dripping onto her shoulders, sending droplets down her torso, over her breasts and back.

She approached him from behind as he was removing a box of condoms from his nightstand and slipped her hands around his waist. When she took his erection in her hand and began massaging him, his breath caught in his throat.

She trailed her tongue along the planes of his back, slid her other hand up his belly to his chest and marveled at how amazing he felt.

If it all hadn't been so damn pleasurable, she might have been able to muster some renewed annoyance that he still wasn't proving to be the cold fish she'd hoped he would be.

He turned to face her. "A little impatient?"

"You were taking too long," she said.

"I wasn't gone for ten seconds."

"I don't believe in sitting around waiting for things to happen." She pushed him backward with the weight of her body, urging him to the bed only a foot away.

"You love to be in control," he said, standing his ground and grasping her wrists, pinning them at her sides.

"So do you." She tossed him a look that was pure challenge.

Not only did she love to be in control, she loved a good fight.

"Therein lies our problem," he whispered, then dipped his head to kiss her.

His kiss was part invitation and part challenge, both coaxing and forceful. Claire let him kiss her for a few moments, then she nipped at his lip with her teeth and pulled away.

"Let go of my wrists," she said, and he did.

She gave him a good shove, and he fell backward onto the bed. Claire climbed on top of him and pinned his arms at his sides.

Mason laughed. "If you think you can hold me like this, you're deluded."

"I think you want me badly enough to put up with whatever I do to you."

"Don't be so sure of yourself—I could say the same about you," he said, grinding his erection against her, nearly driving her insane.

"Let's get this over with," she said, sounding a little more breathless than she would have liked.

He broke free of her hold and toppled her on the bed, pinning her with the weight of his body, holding her wrists the way she'd just been holding his. "Don't talk about having sex with me like it's some kind of chore."

She smirked. "Oh, does that bother you? I'm so sorry."

"*You* bother me."

"I wasn't bothering you on the dance floor, it seems."

"Oh hell yes, you were."

She strained against his hold, but to no avail. And truthfully, it made her even hotter to realize she had no physical control. The only control she might exert was on his mind, and even that would be a challenge given her state of arousal.

"Let go," she halfheartedly demanded. "I thought your note said no more talking."

"I'll shut up when you admit that I gave you the best sex you've ever had," he said with a toying smile she'd never seen him wear before.

"Don't flatter yourself. You were okay," she lied. "You're enjoying this, aren't you?"

"I like a good argument."

"I like less talk and more action," she said.

His hot, hard erection, against her thigh, between her legs, so close to easing her crazy ache, was driving her insane.

He let go of her wrists long enough to put on a condom, then pinned her on the bed again and forced his cock inside her in one delicious thrust.

Claire couldn't help it—she cried out at the relief of having her most urgent desire satisfied.

Mason gave her a hungry kiss, then asked, "Are you going to be good now?"

She strained against his grip, to no avail, and felt herself grow even more aroused by the loss of control. "Hell no."

Claire shot him a look of challenge, arching her back and straining against his weight.

His hips, moving between her legs, stilled. "You want me to stop?" he asked, his voice husky.

"Only when you've finished what you started."

"Then we need to set some ground rules. If I let go of your hands, you can't assault me. No hitting, no scratching, no biting."

His body, enveloped by hers, was doing little now to bring her the release she wanted more than breath. She tightened her muscles around him, hoping he'd get the message, and he closed his eyes and moaned.

"I can't make any guarantees I'll play fair," she said.

"Then neither can I," he nearly growled, and began thrusting into her again.

The friction and force of his cock was exactly what she needed, and she simply let go of everything else, savored each forceful, merciless thrust.

They made love like wild animals, angry and passionate, hungry and frantic. Claire realized this was the first time in her life a man had ever truly dared to dominate her.

And she loved it.

At some point, Mason must have let go of her hands, because now she realized she was clinging to him for dear life as he pushed her closer and closer to climax. She moaned into his mouth as he kissed her, helpless to do anything but lie there and accept him into her, accept his invasion because there was nothing else she wanted more in the world.

And then with all the tension that had built up between them, her release came stronger and harder than she would have imagined possible. She cried out like a wounded animal, though her body felt anything but injured.

Pleasure coursed through her, leaving her weak and limp as Mason found his own release. He moaned into her mouth as he kissed her, embraced her tighter as he spilled into her, possessed her so completely she wasn't sure where she ended and he began.

Finally, she opened her eyes to see him gasping, his gaze pinned on her as he caught his breath.

Then he placed gentle kisses on her nose and cheeks as he relaxed between her legs. His kisses were so tender, so different from their intense encounter, they caused Claire's throat to tighten.

She'd never gotten choked up about sex before, and she didn't intend to let it happen now. She just needed to focus on the facts. This was Mason Walker, a man she could barely stand to be in the same room with when he had his clothes on.

She was *not* supposed to be emotionally moved by him or the sex they had.

But she couldn't conjure up any outrage. The feel of Mason's heat, the weight of his body, obliterated all coherent thought.

He propped his head on one hand and smiled a slow, sexy smile. "Are you cured of me yet?"

Claire couldn't help but smile back. "I'm not sure…. This may take all night."

And that, she feared, was a very conservative estimate.

MORNING LIGHT FLOODED the bedroom. Mason yawned and stretched, his body aching from a night that had tested his physical limits.

He'd always considered himself an enthusiastic lover, but hell—with Claire, enthusiasm seemed too tame a word. He had the sore muscles to prove it. Even with his strenuous daily regimen at the gym, he'd still managed to give himself a hard workout last night. At some point during the night they'd ordered room service and eaten a late dinner in bed, but even still, he'd worked up enough of an appetite with her that he was ravenous now.

He sat up in bed and watched Claire as she slept, her red hair spilling over the pillow and her breasts barely concealed by the white sheet that rose and fell with her chest as she breathed. With her eyes closed and her face tranquil in sleep, she looked like a different woman.

Awake, Claire was all fire and sex appeal. Her eyes, her expressions, her body language, all pointed to the hellion she was.

Asleep, she possessed a peaceful quality that she could never exude while awake. She looked vulnerable even—a quality Mason never would have attributed to Claire.

As if she could feel him watching her, her eyes opened. "Morning," she said, her voice soft.

It was awkward having her here now. He didn't know what to do with Claire if they weren't arguing or having sex.

"I'm a little surprised you didn't sneak out in the middle of the night."

Claire rubbed her eyes and smiled a half smile. "Too tired. You wore me out."

"I think it was the other way around." And even after all they'd done, the sight of her body outlined under the sheet was enough to make him hard again. He adjusted the sheet on his lap to conceal his body betraying him.

"Don't feel obligated to engage in any nicey-nice morning chitchat with me. I think we both know the deal."

Now that was the Claire he knew. And if she wanted to cut to the chase...

"I believe you owe me something now," Mason said.

Claire rolled over to face him, and a lazy smile spread across her lips. "What could I possibly owe you now?"

"The complete story?"

Her smile disappeared. "What complete story?"

"The rest of the information about the dominatrix-for-hire service."

"Oh. Right, I forgot about that."

"Great sex make you forgetful?"

"No one could ever accuse you of being overly modest."

Mason shrugged. He wasn't, but that was beside the point. "So have you gotten tired of me yet?"

She cast a suspicious look at him. "Why do you ask?"

"Wasn't that the whole point of our sleeping together?"

"I thought you were sleeping with me to get information."

"Stop trying to divert attention from my question."

"Yes, you're out of my system, okay? Mission accomplished. Congratulations."

"You don't exactly sound thrilled about it."

"This isn't my idea of great morning-after pillow talk."

"You said no nicey-nice chitchat, right?" Mason decided not to point out that it was her idea in the first place that they sleep together this way. He wasn't so sure the crazy experiment had been even remotely successful for him, but hey—if it got him the information he needed…

She narrowed her eyes at him. "I changed my mind."

Mason resisted smiling at how easily he could ruffle her feathers. "So tell me, what else do you know about this dominatrix ring?"

Claire sat up in bed and crossed her arms over her glorious breasts, so dewy and lush in the soft light, it was all he could do not to lean over and take them into his mouth. "That's all you care about, isn't it? Your damn business. No wonder you're such a success—you know how to put work first, that's for sure."

"I should have known I couldn't trust you to keep a deal."

She smiled sweetly. "You're an asshole."

"So this is how it goes—we can't talk for five minutes without getting in an argument? It's a good thing you're tired of sleeping with me, already."

She shot him a look of death. "Yeah, good thing," she said as she pushed the sheets aside and stood up.

Mason watched her stalk across the room and out the door, presumably in search of her clothes that had been discarded last night in the living room. Her perfect backside, smooth and lush, beckoned him to follow her. As infuriating as she could be, he felt a loss at her absence from his bed.

Last night had been nothing short of incredible. Explosive, amazing, earth-shattering… Overblown adjectives couldn't express how moved he'd been—and still was. Part of him wanted Claire to leave just so he could have the time to examine how he felt, try to explain away the emotion that had welled up in his chest.

And part of him wanted to forget about it, forget her, forget last night. Move on.

But his business side wanted to stalk into the living room after her and demand she tell him what she knew. Which probably wasn't anything he couldn't find out on his own. Still, a deal was a deal.

He got out of bed, grabbed a pair of jeans from the closet and tugged them on.

"Claire, you're not leaving until you tell me what you know."

She was tugging on her dress. "Fine. Maybe I should call a few travel magazines and let them know what's going on here, too."

She was bluffing. He hoped.

"Go ahead. All they'll find is me stopping this thing before it's had a chance to get started."

She jammed her feet into a pair of sexy heels, and Mason found himself momentarily distracted by the sight of her struggling to get the straps of her shoes around her ankles. He forced his brain back into gear.

"Fine, you want to know the rest? That muscle-bound blond bartender at the Cabana Club is involved in it. That's all I know," she said, then turned and headed for the door.

Mike D'Amato? Mason tried to wrap his brain around the possibility. Anything was possible, he'd learned, and even people he considered trustworthy could be snakes in the grass.

"Claire, wait."

"Bye, Mason. Nice knowing you," she said as she opened the door and stepped into the hallway. "Last night was loads of fun," she said in a voice meant to convince him it was anything but.

Mason watched as she closed the door, unable to utter a word or make a move. Why he'd frozen in place, he had no idea. One thing was sure though—Claire leaving was the best thing that could happen to him.

Really, it was.

So he couldn't figure out why her closing the door had felt like a punch in the gut.

6

CLAIRE TURNED ON the water in the shower, then started undressing as she played and replayed the events of the night and morning in her mind.

What the hell was she doing? Here she was at Mason's new resort in the Caribbean, having just spent what was possibly the most incredible night of her life...with a guy who drove her absolutely crazy.

Worst of all, her plan had been an utter, complete, down-and-out failure.

Mason was not out of her system, he was not even the slightest bit of a bore in bed, and she needed to adjust her whole outlook on him as a man.

Sure, he was still a world-class jerk, but he was a world-class jerk with bedroom moves to die for.

All her fantasies starring Mason had been dead-on accurate—had possibly even fallen short of how amazing he actually was in bed—and she had no idea what to do about him.

One thing was sure though, if she left the island now, she'd never be free of the fantasies. More likely, they'd only get worse, fueled on by the memories of their only night together.

Oh yeah, she had it bad for Mason, and instead of leaving on the next plane off the island as she'd planned, she feared what she really needed to do was to stick around long enough to find the cure for him. But it would be all too easy to fall victim to his charms.

Storming out of his suite had been nothing more than a rather immature way for her to put some distance between them so that she could think clearly, and it had surely damaged her chances of getting Mason to help her out with her fantasies anymore.

Claire stepped into the shower and winced at the hot water, then slowly relaxed into it. She felt the twinges and aches of a long night of lovemaking, yet another reminder of Mason's mark on her.

Think, Claire, think.

She had to think clearly about the situation. No more rushing headlong into half-baked plans and finding herself in worse trouble than before.

She always had her best ideas in the shower, but as she shampooed her hair, she realized that this shower only reminded her of last night in Mason's shower during their third round of sex, of how he'd worked her into a lather both literally and figuratively, of how close the shower had come to her tropical rainforest fantasy.

Ten minutes later she was toweling off and no

closer than before to a revelation about how to deal with Mason. Rather, her nerves were on edge and her body aching for his touch again.

She seemed to be insatiable all of a sudden. Even after last night's marathon of sex, she still hadn't had enough.

How much more of Mason would be enough? She'd never lusted after a guy so intensely; this was uncharted territory.

And then she saw her plan before her, clear as day. She had to stay at Escapade until she was sick of Mason. She had to convince him to sleep with her, again and again, until she'd had enough.

He'd clearly enjoyed last night as much as she had, if not more, so convincing him shouldn't have been a problem.

Except for the way they'd said goodbye this morning...

She had to convince him not only that she should stay around, but that they should keep up what they'd started last night.

Definitely a challenge.

Claire dressed in her most convincing outfit, then dried her hair until it was its usual mess of crimson waves. A light layer of lipstick followed by a few finishing cosmetic touches, and she was feeling a tiny bit more confident that she could present her case to Mason.

She had one thing going for her—Mason had to

have felt the strength of their attraction as much as she had. If anyone wanted to continue their liaison for a little while longer, it had to be him.

After grabbing a croissant and some coffee at one of the brunch buffets set up for resort guests, Claire followed the already-familiar route back to Mason's suite. But after knocking on the door twice and waiting, she decided he must have already left for the day. Either that or he was avoiding her—which was entirely possible.

Doubt nagging at her, she tried to think where he might have gone on a dreary, blustery Sunday. The storm center still seemed to be hovering offshore, but the island had gotten fairly well pounded late last night, though she and Mason mostly had been too busy to notice. Some palm trees had lost branches, and the sky was a dark gray that suggested more was to come any time now. The wind whipped at Claire as she wandered back outside, but she didn't mind it—even welcomed it. She loved the ocean scent that permeated the air and the sound of the palm trees rustling overhead.

But where was Mason? He seemed like the work-aholic type who might go to his office on a Sunday, so she set out for Escapade's administrative offices, which were located just inside the main entrance of the resort.

But the longer she walked, the more she became convinced that she would need another bargaining chip to ensure she got what she wanted from Mason. Unlimited access to his bed for a week, she feared, would not come easily after the way she'd behaved this morning.

But what if she were useful to him—both in and out of bed? What if she could help him?

Claire stopped in her tracks.

Surely the Cabana Club wouldn't be open at noon, but maybe she could catch the bartender from last night there prepping for the afternoon and evening crowd. She decided to give it a shot and made a beeline for the bar.

Five minutes later, she was inside the cool darkness of the club, but no one else was in sight. Since the front door was open, she assumed someone was indeed in the back prepping, and she headed for the back of the bar toward the kitchen.

"Can I help you?" a male voice called from inside as her footsteps echoed throughout the silent building.

Claire followed the sound of the voice, and found the bartender named Mike from the night before flipping through what looked like an inventory sheet.

"Actually, you can. We met last night? At the bar?"

He looked her over in a way that was half friendly and half lascivious, then smiled. "Sure, I remember you."

"I'm hoping you can tell me who the man that talked to me was."

His expression turned neutral. "You'll have to be

a little more specific. I see hundreds of people a night out there."

"Maybe early to mid-fifties, tall, gray hair, light blue eyes. He called me Ashley, and you corrected him."

"Oh, Mr. Casey. He's one of our VIP guests. We have some customers who spend more than their share of money here, and they get some special treatment."

"Seemed like you two knew each other for some other reason," Claire pressed.

Something passed over his eyes—suspicion?—but he kept his expression neutral and shrugged. "Nope."

She'd have to work some magic if she wanted to get any further with this guy. But something nagged at her—if the man last night had been a VIP, could it be that part of Mason's special treatment for him was some kind of sex-service-for-hire thing?

Could she trust Mason to tell her the truth? Maybe he had Lucy fooled, and maybe he was sleazier than everyone thought.

He had, after all, been more than ready to have sex with her right there on the dance floor of his own nightclub last night. He hadn't hesitated for a moment.

But then, neither had she.

"Who was Ashley? His date for the evening?"

The bartender shrugged. "It's not my business."

Okay, she needed to try a different tack—one that rarely failed her. She smiled and shifted her hips ever so slightly, changing her body language from guarded to come-hither.

"A funny thing happened last night, you know."

"What's that?"

"I left something for you on the bar, but someone else found it."

He smiled, interested now, as she'd known he would be. Unlike Mason, most men were painfully predictable.

"Oh yeah? What was it?"

"My room number. Imagine my surprise when a middle-aged guy in a diaper showed up instead of you."

Mike the bartender blinked in surprise. "A *diaper?* And nothing else."

"A really big diaper and a raincoat."

"You're joking."

"I wouldn't joke about that."

"Did you let him in?"

"Do I look like the kind of girl who'd go for a guy in a diaper?"

He shrugged. "I've seen quite a bit in the short time I've worked here. It doesn't surprise me the weird stuff people go for."

"It's definitely not my choice of fetishes."

"Whatever floats your boat, babe. That's my motto."

"So that's what you say to women in bed?" she said, feeling a little sleazy now.

He grinned as he lifted a crate of vegetables onto the counter. "You can find out firsthand if you want."

Claire groaned inwardly. She'd need another shower after this conversation. "Tempting offer," she said.

"Mondays are my nights off, if you're still going to be around tomorrow."

"I haven't decided, but I think I will be. Maybe we could meet up for dinner?"

Mike D. eyed her, as if trying to decide whether she was worth suffering through a dinner for. She decided to cut to the chase.

"Listen," she said. "Truth is, I like it rough. I'm sort of a closet sadist, if you know what I mean."

"Like I said, whatever floats your boat," he said, turning to the sink to wash some baby carrots.

"Do you like it rough?"

He turned back to her. "I don't mind an occasional pair of handcuffs, but getting spanked really isn't my thing."

"Know anyone who does go for it?"

His expression turned neutral again. She apparently hadn't done as good a job gaining his trust through sexual banter as she'd hoped. "I'll keep you in mind if I hear of anyone looking for that kind of thing."

"Thanks," she said, ashamed of herself for not having the balls to push further. "I'd appreciate that. I'll be around the bar tonight."

"I'll be here," he said. "Now if you don't mind, I've gotta get this food prepped."

Claire left the club, feeling a mixture of relief at escaping her fake flirtation with the bartender and disappointment at not having gotten the information she wanted.

As she headed for Mason's office, she noted that there was no shortage of guests out determined to have a good time in spite of the lousy weather. Even the beach, visible in the distance, was fairly crowded, and the pool she passed along the way was just as busy as it might have been on a sunny day. She supposed the kind of people who came to Escapade weren't necessarily put off by the threat of a hurricane, probably even considered it an added element of excitement.

Just as she had last night....

Having gotten nowhere with Mike, she decided the best way to get what she wanted from Mason was with the direct approach. She'd tell him she wasn't leaving until she had the relief she needed. And maybe a little heartfelt apology would be in order to smooth over the rough edges she'd left this morning.

The clerks at the reception desk were busy with the mass weekend changeover of guests—many checking out and many arriving—and didn't see her slip into the reception area. She followed a sign that read Administrative Offices down a hallway until she found the door that sported a brass placard with the name Mason Walker engraved on it.

She tapped on the door, and Mason's voice called, "Come in," confirming that her guess about his location was correct.

Claire was about to go in when a woman's voice behind her said, "I'm sorry, miss, but this area is for employees only."

She swung around and smiled at the resort employee. "Oh, I'm a friend of Mason's."

"You can't just come wandering back here and knock on his door like this. You'll need to go back to the reception desk and—"

"There's a huge line out there." Claire reached for the doorknob but the woman inserted herself between Claire and the door.

"You cannot disturb Mr. Walker!"

The door jerked open and Mason stood there looking between the two of them. "What's going on out here?"

"I'm so sorry, Mr. Walker, this woman just—"

Mason gave Claire a look. "It's okay, Janine. I know her."

Janine's bubble burst, she glared at Claire and nodded. "Okay, sir. Sorry to disturb you."

Mason stepped aside and let Claire in. "Maybe you should hire a few armed guards if you really want to keep out riffraff like me."

He closed the door and stood there, his arms crossed over his chest. Clearly ready to send her packing at any moment. "What's up, Claire? What are you doing here?"

"I might ask you the same thing," she said, smiling.

"This is my office."

"You work on Sundays, too? Isn't that a bit extreme?"

Mason leaned against his desk and sighed. "I'm

not going to defend my work habits to you, but no, I don't normally work Sundays unless it's necessary."

"Let me guess. Today there's a certain female you're trying to put out of your head. But it's not working, is it?"

"Not when she won't leave me the hell alone, no."

"I just wanted to let you know I'm not leaving today as planned."

Mason's gaze narrowed almost imperceptibly. "Tomorrow, then?"

"No."

"Because?"

"Because I changed my mind. I owe you an apology—I overreacted to your questions this morning."

He didn't bother to hide his shock, and Claire had to smile. She'd never been good at admitting she was wrong, but for the right cause, she could say anything to get what she wanted.

"Apology accepted, so now you can leave, right?"

"You need my help, Mason."

"I do?"

"I can help you get information from Mike D."

"That's not necessary." Mason's mouth was set, firm, uncompromising. Probably the same expression he used to fire employees and dump girlfriends.

"You're his boss—you're everyone's boss here at the resort. Do you really think anyone will be forthcoming with you about nefarious goings-on among their fellow employees?"

"If they want this resort to be a success, and if they want to keep their jobs, yes."

"That's a little naive, Mason."

"Don't you have some havoc to wreak somewhere?"

"You're not getting rid of me that easily," she said, skirting his desk and closing the distance between them.

"Nothing with you is easy. That much, I've got figured out."

"I was pretty easy last night."

Last night—just the thought of their actions on the dance floor and in Mason's suite made her pulse quicken.

Mason cast a glance at her chest, then back up at her eyes. "Why do you want to stay here? I thought you said you'd had enough of me."

Busted.

"I may have told a little untruth in the heat of the moment."

"You haven't had enough of me?"

Claire licked her lower lip, biding her time. "I'm afraid not."

She hooked her finger through his belt loop and pulled him toward her. He didn't offer much resistance, but instead stood and let their bodies come together. Yet, his arms remained at his sides.

Claire had to look up at him now since he was half

a foot taller than her. She could see trouble brewing in his eyes. Even more trouble than usual.

"Guess your plan wasn't as foolproof as you thought it would be, hmm?"

"Guess not," she said, surprised by the uneasy sound of her own voice. She willed some sass into her next statement. "It might have been poor judgment on my part to think it would only take one night."

"So what are you saying?"

"Maybe we need more like a week."

"We?"

"Don't tell me last night left you completely satisfied—"

"I doubt I could get much more satisfied than I was when I woke up this morning."

"You know what I mean."

He sighed. "Yeah, I do. You really think a week will work?"

"Why wouldn't it? We can't stand each other outside of bed, so a week should be more than enough time. Don't you think?"

"Thinking doesn't seem to be part of this equation."

"Sometimes thinking too hard is a bad idea."

"You're the one who thought one night would do the trick. I'm not sure I can buy your logic."

Claire decided a change of subject would be best. "I'm wondering if you can help me get my reservation extended through next weekend."

Mason gave her a look that said he wasn't sure he wanted her around that long, but he went to his computer and sat down, then began typing. She peered over his shoulder at the reservation system, and a minute later he said, "Done."

"Thanks."

He turned and smiled at her. "I hope you'll be recommending Escapade to your clients at the travel agency."

"So far, so good." She smiled back. "I've found a few members of the staff to be extremely accommodating."

"I can imagine."

Claire sat down on the edge of his desk. "I just saw Mike D. at the Cabana Club. It didn't seem like you'd talked to him or anything."

"You went looking for him?"

"I was hoping to pry some information out of him to bring to you as a peace offering."

Mason frowned, the sexy crinkles around the edges of his mouth deepening. He had such a full, sensual mouth, a mouth made for pleasure....

His voice knocked her out of her daze. "That's very thoughtful of you, but you shouldn't have done it."

Claire shrugged. "No harm done."

Mason leaned back in his leather chair and began to rock, his arms behind his head. "I've been debating all morning how to handle this situation."

"I'm a little surprised you didn't just fire the bartender."

"It might be premature. If I can keep a watch on him, I should be able to find out who else is involved and shut the whole operation down at once."

"Smart thinking."

"How exactly do you suppose you can get any information out of Mike?"

"I'm already working on it. A little flirting can do wonders."

"You not only went looking for him, but you flirted with him?"

"I didn't strip my clothes off or anything."

"Is that a common reaction you have to men?"

She smiled, leaning in and tracing the outline of his rough jaw with her finger. "Only certain ones."

7

CLAIRE'S TOUCH was enough to give Mason a hard-on. He was a basket case.

"Still, that was stupid. You could have gotten yourself in trouble out there," he said, half dreading and half anticipating the fire that would light in her eyes.

He'd never been one to start arguments with women. In fact, he usually avoided conflict at all costs, especially since dealing with his vindictive ex and the Fantasy Ranch fiasco.

But with Claire, his whole approach to the opposite sex had been turned on its head.

"Maybe it was kind of dumb. I promise I won't pull any more crazy stunts if you let me stick around and help you solve your dominatrix problem."

"How do you propose to help?" Mason said, almost afraid to hear the answer.

"I think first off, we need to do a little surveillance."

It sounded like a surprisingly reasonable idea. "Okay, so we'll go to the Cabana Club tonight and watch what goes on."

"You can't just drop into the bar and expect someone to hire a dominatrix in front of you."

"You have any better ideas?" Mason said, pretty sure he wasn't going to like her answer.

"You can wear a disguise." She smiled, and Mason knew he was in trouble.

"You mean like a wig and some funny glasses?"

"Something like that."

"I don't think there's much of a supply of costume gear on the island."

"What about for the shows?"

Oh, right. Escapade regularly flew in actors and other performers to do shows at the resort, and there was a well-stocked costume area backstage at the theater.

"I don't know...."

"Come on, show me where the costumes are."

"This is crazy. I can't go skulking around my own resort dressed up like Elvis."

"Not Elvis. I'm thinking we could go for more of a pimp look. Long fur coat, some platform shoes—"

"Not a chance."

"You are seriously no fun."

"That's not what you were saying last night."

"Please. Don't flatter yourself. I just hadn't gotten laid in a while."

Mason's groin went on alert again at the thought of last night. Yeah, he hadn't gotten laid in a while either, so maybe that was why he was feeling so rabid for Claire. He made a mental note to stop working so hard and pay more attention to his neglected love life.

"Oh yeah? Having trouble finding a guy who can put up with your mouth?"

"I never have trouble finding a guy." She stood up and walked to the door. "Let's go."

"What kind of guys do you date, anyway?"

"Whatever kind I want."

"Seriously. Do they let you take off with their cars whenever you want? Do they put up with all your crap without complaining?"

"I like my men to be the silent, physical type. Short on talk and long on action, if you know what I mean."

"I'm afraid I do." Mason had her pegged. She was the kind of person who liked to stay in control by surrounding herself with people who wouldn't stand up to her.

If she wasn't so damn sexy, she never would have gotten away with such behavior.

"Lead the way to the costumes," Claire said, rising from his desk and heading for the door.

"Have you had lunch yet?"

"No," she said, placing her hand on her nonexistent belly. "Now that you mention it, I'm pretty hungry."

"Let's grab some lunch then."

They headed for the nearest restaurant, where every employee tried not to gawk at the sight of Mason with a woman. So far, he'd avoided dating anyone on the island, so making a public appearance with Claire was sure to cause some gossip.

But he also liked to check out what was happening on his resort as often as possible, so this was his chance to not only sample the food but keep an eye on things in general.

He and Claire managed to eat lunch without a single argument ensuing, and by the time they were finished, he was shocked to realize he'd genuinely enjoyed her company outside of bed.

Probably, she was just on her best behavior to ensure she got what she wanted from him. Within a few days, he fully expected them to be getting on each other's nerves so much she wouldn't be able to find a flight off the island fast enough.

After lunch, they crossed the resort while Mason surveyed what was going on. The storm last night had caused some damage, but the grounds crew had done an excellent job of cleaning up fast.

While there had been some complaints about the weather canceling various events, overall, guests had been pretty relaxed, and complimentary bottles of champagne sent to the unhappy guests had smoothed over any wrinkles. Weather reports suggested the storm still hadn't finished with the island, but Mason was confident his employees could handle whatever came their way.

Fifteen minutes later they were backstage at the theater, sorting through various disguise options, and Claire was having a little more fun at the task than he would have liked.

Standing at a shelf full of wigs on mannequin heads, she held up a wig with a ponytail.

"Hell no. I'm not wearing that."

"Oh, come on. Try it—ponytails are sexy, and it's the same color as your hair." She brought it over to him. "Besides, you're a guy. There's just not a lot we can do to make you look really different."

He let her fit the wig on his head. But when she stood back and took in the sight of him in it, then burst out laughing, he growled and ripped it off.

"Okay, it was a little too girlish. I'll find something better."

Claire went back to rummaging through wigs while Mason sorted through a bin of accessory props. Glasses, beards—none of it was going to look natural on him.

"Hey, look at this one." She produced a short but shaggy medium-brown wig that reminded Mason of one of the Beatles.

"Hmm."

She smiled. "I saw a mullet wig over there. You could wear that one and revive a fashion trend."

"Okay, okay. Let's try the shaggy do."

He bent his head down so that Claire could fit the second wig on him. She looked him over once it was on.

"Not bad. It's got a seventies thing going on."

"I don't think I want to have a seventies thing going on."

"It's just for an hour or so, for one night. For the sake of your business!"

"So what else do I need?"

"Maybe some glasses." She spotted a pair on top of the bin of props. "Like these."

Mason took one look at the glasses and shook his head. Claire put them on him, anyway.

She stood back and surveyed his disguise. "Do you have a silky shirt?"

"Don't you think I'll be a little obvious if I go in there looking like Danny Tario?" He took the glasses off and tossed them aside.

"I saw a guy yesterday dressed just like that—tight pants, shiny polyester shirt open at the collar, tinted glasses, shaggy hair—the works."

It was true people felt free to dress however they really wanted when they came to a place like Escapade. If in their everyday lives they didn't feel comfortable dressing like a pimp or a hoochie-mama even though it was their secret desire, then at Escapade, they could let their real selves hang out.

Sometimes quite literally. The Uninhibited area of the resort was just that—a place to be completely uninhibited, free from the shackles of clothing, free to show the world one's true self, so to speak.

Mason wasn't into nudism, but a lot of people were, judging by the popularity of the Uninhibited side.

Nor was he into dressing like a pimp. "I don't know, Claire."

"How about if I dress up, too? It could be fun."

"Dress up how?"

She grinned. "I saw a skimpy little silver slip dress over there that might be fun."

Mason walked over to a rack of women's costumes and began flipping through them. When he came to the ones for a Las Vegas-style show, complete with tassled bras and a fringed skirt that left almost nothing to the imagination, he smiled at Claire.

"How about this?"

"Um, no."

"So there's actually a limit to what you'll do to get attention?"

She crossed her arms and gave him a look. "You know, we're supposed to be going incognito. How can we do that if we look like a couple of freaks?"

"Exactly my point about the pimp-wear."

"Okay, okay. Just wear the wig and some glasses with what you've got on."

She went to the wigs and surveyed them. "I'll need a decent disguise, too, since Mike D. already knows me. Maybe we'll need a whole assortment of costumes to conduct our surveillance this week."

"You've been hanging around Judd and Lucy too much. I'll have this problem dealt with by tomorrow, Tuesday at the latest. We're not going to become amateur sleuths."

"You're such a spoilsport."

"I think it'd be plenty sporting if you'd wear that showgirl costume."

She smiled. "I've worn more interesting outfits than that to the grocery store. If it's entertainment you want, just give me a chance."

She selected a long, straight platinum-blond wig from the shelf and went to a mirror to try it on. Mason watched as she transformed herself from a fiery redhead into a hot, trashy porn star.

"Nice," he said, his body warming at the sight of her looking so delicious in a whole new way.

She turned and surveyed him from head to toe. "Don't get yourself all worked up unless you intend to do something about it."

"I thought we were on our way to solve the great dominatrix-for-hire mystery?"

Not that he wouldn't mind a little diversion on the way, but the temptation to taunt Claire was irresistible.

"I'm game for anything," she said as she closed the distance between them, her hips moving in a way that made him think of sex. "Things won't really get rolling at the bar for another hour, at least, don't you think?"

She was probably right. While the bad weather would send people to the bars early today, it would be at least a little while after lunch before any sort of crowd would gather.

She was standing only inches from him now, and her pink beaded tank top was flimsy enough that he could rip it off with one good tug if he really wanted to. She wasn't wearing a bra underneath, and yet her breasts were full, lush—mesmerizing in their unencumbered state.

He slipped his fingers in the waist of her white capri pants and tugged her against him. "Somebody could walk in on us here."

"Privacy was the last thing on your mind last night." She gazed up at him with a blatant challenge in her eyes.

"Last night was a one-time exception. Maybe this door locks."

"I locked it when we came in here."

"So you planned this all along?"

"I know how men react to blond wigs."

"You're kidding, right?"

"It may sound crazy, but it's true. It plays into that guy fantasy of having a different woman for every day of the week."

"Hmm." He wasn't going to deny that the fantasy existed, but he was pretty damn sure the woman inside the wig had a hell of a lot more to do with his erection than the wig itself.

"This whole theater setting, you know—it makes me think of directors, desperate actresses, compromising positions...."

Mason slid his hands around her waist to her ass and pressed her hips against him. "What sort of compromising positions?"

Her voice grew breathy. "Like, maybe I need to give you something to get that private-investigator part I want so desperately."

Mason watched as she licked her lips, slid her hands up his chest and around his shoulders, then took one of the buttons of his shirt into her mouth. Before he could stop her, she'd bitten it off and was going for a second one.

"Don't you know how to unbutton a shirt?" he said, though he could hardly give a damn if she cut his shirt off with a machete, so long as they got down to business.

"Sorry, I was just trying to demonstrate my acting skills. Guess I got a little carried away."

Mason couldn't help the smile that played on his lips. He had to give Claire credit—she knew how to spice up just about any situation. "You know your part will have some nude scenes. I'll need to see your body, make sure it's camera-worthy."

He pushed her tank top down to reveal her breasts, then took them both into his hands.

"What do you think?" she asked. "Would you call them camera-worthy?"

"Very nice," he said. "More than suited to be the stars of the show."

"I'm glad you like what you see," she said, unzipping his pants and slipping her hand inside.

"I'll need to see a performance from you, too."

Claire gripped his cock and massaged gently. "I hope you don't mind my taking a few liberties. This helps me get into my role."

"I'll bet. You take whatever liberties you want." His voice was tight now, his head starting to spin at the arousal building up inside him.

They'd just been together last night, and already he was so desperate for Claire it was as if they'd never had sex before.

"I do my best work sitting down," she said, withdrawing her hand from his pants, then leading him to a nearby table.

"I'm looking forward to seeing your performance."

"I think you're gonna like it." She urged him onto the table and took his cock out of his pants.

Mason found a condom in his wallet, removed the wrapper and slipped it on as she undressed, leaving only her blond wig and her high-heeled sandals on.

"Nice costume," he said as she climbed on his lap.

Her erect pink nipples, her narrow waist and hips, the delicious triangle of auburn curls at the apex of her legs—it was all Claire.

Utterly irresistible.

And yet the wig threw a whole new dimension

into the excitement. Not only that, but his own disguise made him feel as if he really were someone else, a sleazy director on the set of some B-movie.

When she mounted him, he groaned low in his throat as her tight, wet opening took him in and brought immeasurable pleasure to his body.

"I'm sorry, I forgot to ask your name," he said, gasping as she began to move her hips.

She closed her eyes as her breath came out in short, gasping breaths. "Ginger," she said between gasps, "because I wasn't always a blond."

Mason grasped her hips as he leaned back against the wall, stilling her so that he could thrust his cock deeper, harder, faster into her. He couldn't get enough.

Her breasts bounced with each thrust. Mason watched, loving the sight, loving the feel of her, loving that she could be so nasty, so adventurous, so ready for anything. She slid one hand down her torso and slipped her fingers between her legs, then began pleasuring herself. Soon her gasps turned into throaty moans that mingled with Mason's own.

He didn't hear a key turning in the lock, nor did he hear the door open, and Claire must not have, either. They both froze at the sound of a strange male voice in the room.

"What the—" the voice said, and they looked toward it to see a janitor standing in the doorway gaping at them. "No guests allowed in here!" he said. "You two need to take your hanky-panky somewhere else."

Mason opened his mouth to speak, but no words came to mind.

"I'll give you two minutes to get dressed and get out of here, and then I'm coming back in to clean."

He stepped out and slammed the door. Claire and Mason looked at each other at the same instant, and if he weren't mistaken, he would have sworn she was blushing. Now there was a first.

She exhaled a ragged sigh and collapsed against him. "Oops," she whispered.

"Yeah." She withdrew from him, and Mason groaned. "Do we have to stop?"

"I'm not performing for an audience of more than one," she said as she climbed off his lap.

His desire barely quelled, he disposed of the condom while she gathered up her clothes. His body was tense with frustration, his erection still rock-hard.

"Maybe we should go back to my room," he said, tucking himself back into his pants and zipping up.

Claire glanced at a little gold watch on her wrist. "We really should get down to the bar now, don't you think?"

"I don't know if I can focus on anything until we've finished this," he said.

She came close and gave him a quick kiss. "You'll be okay. Just think of this as a little preview of tonight's events."

"Only if you can guarantee there'll be no more interruptions to the show."

She looked down at herself as she was pulling her pants up. "Oh no! Mike D. might recognize this as the outfit I was wearing earlier today when I talked to him."

She hurried over to the rack of costumes and snatched the silver slip dress off a hanger, then changed into it. Mason watched in agony, unable to look away from the delicious sight of her no matter how much pain it caused him.

Both dressed, they headed for the door. "Don't forget your glasses," Claire said as she shoved her outfit into her purse.

Mason sighed, picked up the cheesy circa 1979 glasses and put them on. A glance in the mirror confirmed that he looked like a B-movie director or maybe a two-bit pornographer.

"Perfect," she said. "Now let's get out of here."

8

CLAIRE TOOK MASON'S HAND and led him out past the janitor, and for at least that moment Mason was glad to be in his disguise. He definitely didn't need rumors of his having sex with women all over the resort leaking out and becoming the main topic of gossip among his employees.

The janitor glared at them as they passed, then called after them, "You two take the fooling around back to your hotel room if you don't want people walking in on you."

Mason made a mental note to have his managers send out staff reminders that guests caught in compromising positions should be treated as gingerly as possible. The resort policy wasn't to scorn minor offenses, instead to offer gentle reminders to keep their more intimate activities relegated to private areas.

Outside, wind from the passing storm was strong enough that they both had to fear for their wigs. Holding on to them as if they were hats threatening to fly off, Mason and Claire hurried through fat drops of rain to the Cabana Club, where Mike D. was scheduled to work again tonight.

Guests were just beginning to fill the club, but Claire and Mason found two seats at the bar together where they had a prime view of the bartender at work.

"What can I get you?" he asked when he saw them.

There was no reason he should have recognized either of them, but Mason still felt a ridiculous sense of relief when he didn't.

They placed their drink orders, and Mason asked for an appetizer platter for them to split when he realized all his pent-up sexual energy was making him hungry.

"So," Claire said when Mike D. went to the other side of the bar. "I guess we should have done some planning ahead of time about how to handle this."

"I'll do the talking. We'll wait and watch for a while, and then I'll approach Mike D. with an inquiry about any underground services the resort might offer."

"You don't think that will be risky? What if he recognizes you?"

"In this getup? He's only seen me face-to-face a few times. We're not all that familiar with each other."

But speak of being recognized… Carter Cayhill stood on the other side of the bar, talking to a waitress. Mason turned away from him, making a mental note to call Carter later and let him know he wouldn't be at the gym for the next few days. At least not until he'd recovered from all the bedroom workouts he was getting with Claire.

"Look over at the other side of the bar," he whispered to Claire. "At the blond guy in the white polo. Tell me when he leaves."

Claire shrugged. "Okay." She watched for a few moments. "He's walking out the door right now."

Mason relaxed and looked around, only to see that they were getting quite a bit of attention. Or at least Claire was.

The only hair color more attention-getting than red was platinum blond, and the men in the club were taking notice of Claire in a big way. Mason preferred her red hair with its uncontrollable waves that fell around her face and managed to look feminine and sultry at the same time. The blond wig was sexy, but not quite as much.

"Men are staring at you," he said, leaning in and whispering in her ear.

"So what else is new?" She flashed a wry grin. "Does it bother you?"

"No, but the way a few of them are staring is a little offensive."

"They're guys. What do you expect?"

"In case you haven't noticed, I'm a guy, too."

"Believe me, I've noticed." She leaned in close and

licked his earlobe at the same time her hand made its way across his thigh and cupped his package.

"No toying with me. I'm already in pain from that incident with the janitor."

"The anticipation will just make tonight more fun."

"'Fun' isn't the word I'd choose," Mason said as his body grew more tense from her teasing. He shifted on the bar stool.

Mercifully, Claire moved her hand back to his thigh. "You poor men, so ruled by your penises."

"I've only got one penis, and I'm in complete control of it."

Claire laughed.

"You're not in any sort of agony from having been interrupted?"

"Of course I am, but I can take it when I know I'll eventually get what I want."

A rumbling from the sky could be heard from outside, even over the too-loud Caribbean music a band was playing on the other side of the bar. Then came a loud clap of thunder and the lights flickered. Rain must have begun to pour outside because a rush of wet guests came into the club, and a moment later the lights went out completely.

Mason sat there unsure what to do. If he put on his resort-owner cap and went to check the extent of the power outage, he'd risk blowing his cover. But if he sat here, he'd risk someone mishandling the situation and having upset guests with ruined vacations.

Claire looked around the dark club and sighed. "I doubt we're going to see much of anything now."

"I'm thinking I should go check out the problem and make sure it's being handled."

Claire's grip on his thigh tightened. "Don't you have people to take care of stuff like that?"

"Yeah, but this is a first for the resort. People may not be familiar with procedures yet." But she was right, and he did trust his managers for the most part to handle the problem.

The music had stopped. Around them, people were talking and laughing nervously. The club had taken on the hushed tone that always followed a power outage, as if people were afraid talking too loudly would keep the power from coming back on.

Emergency lights kept the club at least dimly lit, enough that people didn't have to bump into each other to get around. The lights showed the way to the exits, and normal procedure for a power outage was for people to be evacuated from the building.

Employees gathered at the bar, and Mason could hear them discussing that very issue when the lights flickered and came back on.

The club manager appeared on stage. "Thanks for your patience, everyone. We're thinking either the storm's hitting the island hardest right now or else there are too many people using the hot tubs at the same time." People laughed, and he continued. "So let's get this party rolling."

The music started up again, and the atmosphere in the club changed instantly back to its former level of joviality.

"Close call," Claire said.

"Who knows if that's the end of the problem though."

A few minutes later, Mike D. set their drinks on the bar, and soon after a waitress came with their appetizer platter.

"Mmm, thanks for thinking of food. All this sexual anticipation's making me hungry."

Claire picked up a shrimp and dipped it in mango sauce, then took her time biting into it as she kept her gaze fixed on Mason. He felt his groin stir and decided if he didn't get Claire out of his system and off his island soon, he'd go insane.

They devoured the appetizers and ordered a second platter, all the while keeping their eyes peeled for any nefarious goings on. But no luck. After an hour and a half at the bar, they both agreed that they needed to tackle the problem more directly.

"You sure you want to do this?" Claire asked. "I can do the asking."

"Thanks, but I think it's more convincing if I do it."

He caught Mike D.'s attention and motioned him over.

"What can I get for you? Another round?" the bartender asked when he reached them.

"Actually," Mason said, leaning in close and

speaking as low as possible over the sound of "Red, Red Wine" being played by the band. "I was hoping to order something that's not on the menu."

Mike D. gave him a speculative look. "If I know how to make it, it's yours."

"Not a drink."

"What then?"

"I've heard there are special services to be had here for the right price."

"Oh yeah? Who'd you hear that from?" The bartender's tone was more suspicious than helpful. Mason clearly hadn't earned his trust, nor had he expected to so easily.

He produced a fifty-dollar bill from his wallet and placed it on the bar, then slid it across to him.

"For information," Mason said. "I'm looking for a little third-party companionship for my girlfriend and I, if you know what I mean."

The bartender's expression softened. "I think your meaning's becoming clear to me." He picked up the money and tucked it in his chest pocket. "What kind of companionship are you interested in?"

Mason tried his best to look like a sleazebag. "A little S and M action, maybe?"

"For you or for the lady?" He nodded at Claire, who was doing her best to look bored.

"For her," he said. "I like to watch."

Mike D. nodded. "Got it. Who told you you'd find something like that here?"

"Another guest at the resort. One of your happy customers."

"I'll need your name and room number, plus five hundred dollars cash up front."

He could have ended the conversation right there and fired Mike D. on the spot, but he wanted to see just how much information he could gather and how many of his employees might be involved. For all he knew, this was just the tip of the iceberg.

He withdrew five hundred from his wallet.

"Whoa, man," the bartender whispered. "No big money exchanged over the counter. You gotta wait till I bring you your bill. Then pay for the drinks and the other stuff at the same time. Got it?"

"Oh, right man."

"And write your information on a napkin and put it inside the bill folder, too."

Mason nodded. "Got it."

Mike D. left to deal with another customer, and Claire gave Mason a look. She leaned in. "You're actually going to hire a dominatrix?"

"How else will I know who's performing the service?"

"Oh, I don't know—ask Mike D. once he's busted?" she said, her tone making it clear she wasn't ready to play S and M games with another girl.

"You weren't so afraid to get it on with a woman last night."

"Screw you."

"Exactly."

"You know I was just toying with you. I am *so* not into chicks. Especially not scary chicks in leather and spikes."

"Damn, you just spoiled my fantasy."

She rolled her eyes and propped her elbows on the bar. "Can you remind me of exactly why I'm helping you in the first place, because I sure as hell can't remember."

A burly bald guy sat down on the other side of Claire and offered her a flirtatious smile. She tossed her faux-blond hair over her shoulder and smiled back.

Mason felt an unexpected wave of possessiveness well up inside his chest.

"Hi. You here alone?"

Claire said nothing for a moment. "You might say that," she finally purred.

Mason leaned in and placed his arm on the back of her bar stool. "Or you might say she's here with me, and then you'd be right."

"Doesn't seem like the lady wants to be here with you."

Was he actually having this conversation and the two that had come before, or had he just stepped into somebody else's crazy life when he put on the bad wig and the glasses?

"Trust me, I'm the one she'll be leaving with."

"I think she's the one gets to decide that," he said, then looked at Claire. "You want to dance, pretty lady?"

She tossed Mason a look that dared him to stop her and said, "Actually, I'd love to."

He resisted the urge to pick her up, throw her over his shoulder and carry her back to his suite caveman-style.

Instead, he shot Claire a look and downed his vodka. What he needed was a double.

"Hey," the guy next to Claire said. "You got a problem with the lady dancing with me?"

He was standing up now, coming over to Mason.

"Looks like you're the one with the problem," Mason said as he set his glass on the bar and stood up.

Actually, Mason was clearly the more screwed of the two. If he got in a fight now, his wig would go flying off and blow his cover. Over Macho Man's shoulder, he could see Claire gloating, clearly enjoying her revenge.

He made a mental note to give her a good hard spanking when he finally got her alone.

The guy with the overdose of testosterone gave him a shove. "You think so? Let me show you the problem I'm talking about."

The jerk-off drew back his fist, and Mason was preparing to duck, when a bottle shattered on the bald guy's head. He swung around to find Claire looking barely apologetic.

"Sorry, but I'm not gonna dance with you if you beat up my date."

"You bitch."

"Okay, I'm definitely not dancing with you now. I like to stick with fully evolved humans."

The bald guy was bleeding from the scalp, rubbing his head as beer dripped onto his shoulder.

"It's time for you to leave," Mason said, feeling completely inadequate for being more worried about his wig than he was about Claire's honor.

A bouncer Mason had never met before finally noticed the situation and appeared beside them. "What's going on here?"

"This asshole's insulting my girlfriend and trying to start a fight."

"Looks like he's the one with the injury."

"I had to do something to stop him from hitting my Jakey," Claire said in a baby-doll voice he'd never heard her use before. She batted her eyelashes, Little Miss Innocent now—though she didn't do innocent very convincingly.

"I think you need to step out, dude," the bouncer said to Macho Man. "I'm sure you'll have a better time at one of the other clubs on the island."

"What the hell? I wasn't doing nothing wrong!"

"Come on, man. And you should probably drop by the clinic and make sure you don't need any stitches on that cut."

Mason and Claire watched as the bouncer led the guy out of the Cabana Club by the elbow.

Mason looked at Claire when the coast was clear. "What, exactly, were you trying to do there? Test me?"

She smiled. "No, just issuing you a warning. Don't screw with me, and don't ever try to set me up to get freaky with a dominatrix. I can make life complicated for you."

"Trust me. I figured that out the first time we met."

"Apparently not."

"You don't really think I expect you to act out an S and M show in front of me, do you?"

"How the hell should I know? You're the one hiring her."

Mason glanced down at the bar and noticed that Mike D. had delivered their check inside a black leather bill folder. He opened it and found their bill along with a pen.

"You won't have to do a thing, I promise. That is, until after she leaves. And what's with calling me 'Jakey,' by the way?"

"Oh," she grinned. "It's just the first name that popped into my head."

"Anyone I should know about?"

"I don't know a single guy named Jake. I promise."

He withdrew the money from his wallet and tucked it into the leather folder, then took a drink napkin from the bar and wrote his new fake first name, Jake, along with his own last name, Walker, which was common enough not to matter. Then he wrote Claire's room number beneath it.

When Mike D. appeared again, he slid the leather folder across the bar to him.

The bartender opened it, eyed the money, and closed it again. "All right man, you're set. I can have your drink order to you by nine o'clock."

Mason nodded, his gut a weird swirl of emotions. Fury that his own employees were conducting illegal activities on his resort. Excitement that he was finally going to get Claire alone again. And dread that once he had her alone, once he'd had his way with her, it still wouldn't be enough.

9

CLAIRE DIDN'T KNOW what to do with Mason alone inside her hotel room, with a dominatrix-for-hire possibly showing up at any moment. It was one of those awkward situations where conversation seemed inappropriate, but hopping into bed seemed premature for once in their bizarre little relationship.

Mason was lounging on her bed in his bad wig and his even-worse glasses, still managing to look damn sexy in spite of the disguise. He was thumbing through her copy of *Chloe* magazine, pausing to admire the scantily clad women and chuckling over the articles about sex and how to please men in bed.

"You actually read this?" he said.

"No, I just buy it for the pretty pictures. What do you think?"

"I think you don't need any of these lame sex tips. You're pretty far advanced past the it's-okay-to-make-sexy-sounds-in-bed stage."

She couldn't help but smile. "I didn't realize anyone needed to be told to make sex noises."

"According to the editors of *Chloe* magazine, you're wrong."

She stretched out on the bed beside him and started reading over his shoulder. "Oh, and it's okay to touch myself?"

"Do you need my permission?"

"It says right there, 'Guys like it when a woman takes the initiative to help work herself toward an orgasm. And the sight of you touching yourself will get him hotter than ever.'"

Mason gave her a speculative look. "I think you proved their theory today."

"It's no theory," she said, elbowing him. "There's not a straight guy on earth who doesn't love to see a woman masturbating."

"I can't argue with that."

"What other gems of advice do they have in there?" Claire tried to keep reading, but having Mason so close, so warm, so right-there-on-her-bed, was a bit of a distraction.

Even more distracting was the realization that she'd spent the entire afternoon with him and had thoroughly enjoyed herself. Aside from the janitor interruption and the incident with the big bald guy, she couldn't think of the last time she'd had so much fun out of bed.

And maybe she'd overreacted to the dominatrix thing a bit by flirting with the bald guy. Definitely a poor judgment call on her part, but Mason had behaved admirably, and she'd loved that he hadn't been chomping at the bit to be a tough guy.

"So, um, were you worried about your wig falling off earlier?" she asked, barely able to keep from giggling.

"What are you talking about?"

"You know, when that bald guy was harassing us."

He was silent for a moment, and then she noticed his abdomen quaking with silent laughter. That sent her over the edge, and she erupted in a fit of giggles.

Her own wig was hot and itchy, and she couldn't wait to rip it off and hurl it across the room. As she laughed, it got knocked askew and half her platinum-blond hair hung in front of her face.

Mason got control of himself. "Here, let me fix that for you." He reached for her wig, but she pulled away.

"Don't you know it's impolite to adjust a woman's wig?"

His own wig was sitting cockeyed on his head, giving him a vague resemblance to a Muppet—a sexy Muppet, but still a Muppet. Claire's laughter erupted all over again, and she fell back on the bed.

"What?" he said, feeling his wig and adjusting it back to its proper position. "Hasn't anyone ever told you it's rude to laugh at a man's hairpiece?"

"Sorry," she said. "I know how sensitive you guys can be about that stuff."

Mason stretched out beside her where she'd flopped back on the bed. "There's a quiz in here they say you're supposed to share with the guy in your life. I guess that's me, at least for tonight, huh?"

Claire rolled her eyes. "I refuse to be rated by one of those quizzes. I don't care what the subject is."

He read the title, "'What's your Sex-Q?' I guess that's like your IQ, but for—"

"I got it."

"You don't want to know what your Sex-Q is? Or what mine is?"

"I think I have a pretty good idea already."

He tossed the magazine aside and smiled. "You've got a great laugh," he said. "Very girlish. Sexy."

"Oh yeah?"

He was looking at her mouth, and Claire realized then how badly she was aching for him, how badly she wanted him to cover her body with his and kiss her senseless.

"Yeah," he said, about to kiss her.

There was a knock at the door, and they looked at each other at the same time as if to silently say "Uh-oh."

"The dominatrix," Claire whispered. "We didn't even talk about how to handle her!"

"I'll just tell her we changed our minds—or better yet, that you got pissed at me for wanting to join in on the action and now you're refusing to go through with the threesome," he whispered.

"Oh sure, pin the blame on me."

Mason stood up from the bed and checked his

wig and glasses in the mirror, then made adjustments before going to the door.

When he opened it, there was a woman in a black coat standing there holding a black duffel bag. Claire was pretty sure she didn't want to know what was in the bag.

"Hi, Mike D. told me to come."

"Oh, right," Mason said, affecting a sort of "dude" accent that Claire struggled not to giggle at. "We got a problem here with my woman."

"I need to come inside. I can't just be standing around out here looking conspicuous."

"Oh, right." Mason stepped aside. "Come on in."

He tossed what Claire supposed was meant to be a reassuring look at her, but she was still not keen on having this situation in her hotel room.

"The thing is," he said after closing the door, "My girlfriend doesn't want to do what we hired you for."

Claire studied the woman's features in case she needed to recall them later. She was thin, probably pretty under her heavy makeup, with dark brown hair and brown eyes. Her nose had a little bump from a previous break, and she looked more like a woman playing dress-up as a dominatrix than an actual whip-wielding pro. Claire supposed it would be pretty difficult to get top-of-the-line dominatrix services on a remote private island in the middle of the Caribbean.

The woman looked dumbfounded. "Um, I can still do it with you."

"Sorry, babe. I'm pretty sure she'll have me swimming with the sharks if I do that," he said as he jerked his thumb toward Claire on the bed.

She did her best to look pissed off and pouty. "You better freakin' believe I will."

"You know, there are no refunds," the woman said.

"No big deal. I'll just take it out of her allowance. She'll have to stop shopping for a few weeks to pay for not doing girl-sex for me."

Claire picked up a pillow and threw it at him, hoping she was doing a convincing job of being the jealous girlfriend. "Screw you!"

"Whatever. I'm out of here then."

"Hey, um, I didn't catch your name."

The dominatrix offered a little smile. "I'm Madame Giselle."

"Oh," Mason said in his dude accent. "Is that like, your stage name or something?"

"Something like that," she said.

"Well, can I just call you Giselle?"

"Sure."

Claire crossed her arms over her chest and glared at them. "And how about I call *you* my *ex*-boyfriend?"

"Hey, what's with the attitude? I'm just talkin' to the lady, okay? Can't I treat her like a human being?"

Claire grabbed the magazine from the bed and pretended to flip through it. "Whatever!"

Mason turned back to Madame Giselle. "Hey, since she's bein' such a bitch, and I've already paid for your time, you mind just hanging out and talking for a little while?"

"Um, I don't think your girlfriend's gonna like that," she said, glancing nervously over at Claire, who was peering at her out of the corner of her eye.

"Ignore her. She's got her panties in a wad or something. I'm thinking she ought to go play in the storm tonight."

"Okay." She shrugged. "I can stick around. It's your money."

Mason motioned to the dinette and chairs near the window, and Giselle sat down there with him. Claire wasn't sure exactly what she was supposed to do now in this weird little tableau, but she knew Mason had seen his chance to grill the dominatrix for information. Claire was torn—should she storm out, lock herself in the bathroom like a jealous girlfriend, or stick around to help remember details of their conversation?

She opted for staying in the room and eavesdropping. After all, if Mason really had been her boyfriend, she supposed one sensible reaction would be to want to stick around and make sure nothing went on between her guy and the hired help.

"So," Mason said. "How'd you end up in this line of work?"

Madame Giselle gave him an odd look. "I majored in sexual domination in college—what do you think?"

"Come on now, seriously. How do you end up

doing this kind of work, and all the way out here on some tiny island?"

She shrugged. "I've got a day job here, too. Trust me, this doesn't pay the bills."

"Huh. That surprises me. You have to give a big cut of the money to that Mike guy at the bar?"

She crossed her arms over her chest and sighed. "I really can't discuss details with you—sorry."

"Hey, babe. No biggy. I'm just curious." He pushed his glasses up on his nose, and Claire almost lost her composure. She stared hard at the What's Your Sex-Q? article to keep from laughing.

"It's okay."

"It must suck having to pay some guy when you do all the work, huh?"

She tossed him a suspicious look. "What are you? Some kind of undercover cop or something? I'm out of here," she said and rose from the table.

"Wait! I'm not a cop." Mason followed her across the room to the door.

"You got a problem, you take it up with Mike D." She opened the door and stalked out, not even bothering to say goodbye.

Mason closed the door and exhaled. "Guess I blew that one, huh?"

"I thought you did pretty well, considering." She tossed the magazine aside and went to him.

"I didn't even find out her real name or where she works at the resort."

"Don't you have photos on file of all your employees?"

"Yeah, but it'll take a while to sort through them just to find one person."

"We can also keep an eye out for her when we're out and about."

"Right." He pulled her to him and locked his hands around her hips. "The important thing is, we're alone again."

"Hmm, I thought the important thing was saving your resort from crazed dominatrixes."

"Not a chance."

"So what makes you think I don't still have my panties in a wad?"

Mason smiled down at her. "In a couple of minutes you won't be wearing your panties, so it doesn't matter if they are or not."

"You sound pretty confident."

"A guy with my looks and charm," he said, then paused to comb back his shaggy wig hair with his fingers. "I can't be anything *but* confident."

"Does this mean we can take off our disguises?"

Mason reached for Claire's wig and pulled it off, much to her relief. She fluffed her hair and scratched at her scalp.

"Say goodbye to Ginger," she said.

"And let's don't forget our farewell to Jake." He took off the glasses and wig, and Claire rose up on tiptoes to give him a kiss.

She brushed his lips with hers, then said, "I'd rather say hello to you."

"Thank you for helping me out today," he said.

Claire smiled, not willing to take any of this too seriously. "Hey, you know the price for my help."

"Let's see… What was it you wanted? A rowboat to get off the island?"

Claire gave him a playful smack on the chest. "Sex, babe. I want your sex."

"Oh yeah, it's all coming back to me now."

"So are you going to give me what I want, or will I have to take it?"

Mason slid his hands up her torso, grazing her breasts through the slinky fabric of the silver dress. "I think I can accommodate you," he said as he teased her nipples.

That's all she was asking for—a little accommodation. And maybe tonight would be the night she got enough of him. Maybe she'd wake up in the morning ready to leave, rid herself of Mason, walk away and never see him again.

But with his hands dipping inside her dress, caressing the bare flesh of her breasts, she had to admit it didn't seem very likely at the moment.

MASON CARRIED HER to the bed and freed her of the trashy little silver dress. Their mouths collided then, an edge of desperation hurrying them forward as she helped him out of his own clothes.

All the tension that had built up inside him since they'd been interrupted by the janitor threatened to come bursting forth, and Mason couldn't remember ever having felt so desperate for release. He ached for Claire right down to his bones.

He tumbled onto the bed with her and kissed wherever his mouth met flesh, tasted, felt, explored…

Claire wound up on top of him, her soft naked body molding to him, driving him to the brink of insanity. She pushed herself up, straddling him, her hot, wet center molding to his cock.

Mason sighed. Closed his eyes. Savored the sweet agony.

"I just realized, I don't have any condoms here."

His eyes shot open. "I used the one in my wallet earlier."

Her stricken expression must have matched his own. "Damn it."

"You have some in your suite?"

"Let's go." He shot up, pulled her off the bed, and they fumbled with their clothes, dressing haphazardly without bothering to worry about underwear or straight buttoning jobs.

A few minutes later they were racing across the resort in the rain, hand in hand, drawing occasional stares from other passing couples who were out braving the weather for one reason or another.

The tropical storm whipped at them and soaked them but was hardly a deterrent. A full-blown hurricane couldn't have stopped Mason from his goal then.

The way Claire made him feel was dangerous, insane, out of control, and he couldn't wait to finish with her and get back to his easy, controlled existence. He liked predictability. He craved order. And he prided himself on his levelheadedness. All that flew out the window when Claire was around.

He wanted his life back.

But at the moment, it was hard to care about anything except finding the nearest condom so he could bury himself deep inside her over and over until the aching stopped.

They made it to his suite in record time and let themselves in, breathless and soaked. His hand gripping Claire's, he tugged her to the bedroom. Again they undressed in a hurry, and Mason went to his nightstand and found the box of condoms. His hands fumbling with the lid, he tore the box open and flung the little black packets all over the bed.

Not exactly like a bed of roses, but it was the best he could do in his half-crazed state.

He pinned Claire on the bed, condoms surrounding her. "Hopefully we won't run out."

She laughed. "If we do, a lack of protection will be the least of our worries."

Mason covered her mouth with his, too desperate to wait a second longer, thrust his tongue inside her mouth and drank her in, but a kiss could hardly quench his thirst. He needed her now.

He sat up and pulled her up with him. Claire opened a condom and slid it on him, and he turned her around and grasped her hips. His cock, pressed against her, so close to entering her, was almost all he could focus on.

He slid his hands around her waist, then let one slip between her legs. She was so wet, so ready....

He found one of her breasts with his other hand and squeezed her nipple while he kissed the back of her neck and rubbed her clit. She moaned, squirmed her hips against him.

"Please," she whispered. "I want you inside me."

He'd intended to practice a tiny bit of self-control to make sure she got hers first, but it only took that one breathy little request to break down his will.

Bending her over, he held firm on her hips and pushed into her from behind. She arched her back and accepted him as deep as he could go, and it was as if a dam had broken.

Mason could no longer take his time. He thrust into her, faster and faster, harder and harder, until he was trembling, blind, sweating.

He could hear his own gasping breaths, could feel his body tensing in preparation for a great release, and then it came.

He came. His body was out of his control as he spilled into her, holding on tighter to her than he should have, unable to let go as the blinding pleasure coursed through him, out of him.

And then he collapsed over her, showered kisses on her back. Mason slipped his hand down between her legs, and with his cock still inside her, he found her clit and massaged her until she too climaxed.

Her cries of pleasure drowned out the sound of his breathing as her body bucked against his touch. When her muscles stopped flexing, he slowed the massage, then stopped. Held her tight. Lowered her to the bed. Curled his body against her.

They lay like that together for a while until the chill of the air-conditioning got to Mason and he sat up to pull the covers over them. Part of him was ready for another round, and part of him was content just to lie still and enjoy the silence with Claire.

But silence made him start thinking. About Claire. About their crazy weekend. About what they were doing together.

"When is it going to be enough?" he whispered, half to himself, not expecting an answer.

Claire's breathing had grown slow and steady, and he didn't really expect her to still be awake. Tucked up against him, warm and soft in his arms, was where she seemed to belong at that moment. It was hard to imagine this was just a temporary thing when she felt so right.

"I don't know," she said.

"I thought you might be asleep."

"Maybe we just need another couple of days."

"Yeah," he said. "I hope you're right."

As soon as he said it, he wished he could suck the words back into his mouth. It had come out sounding bad.... And yet, he couldn't deny it, could he? He didn't want Claire around any longer than necessary, right?

If he wasn't mistaken, he could feel her body stiffen against him, but she said nothing.

Because she felt the same way, of course. She wanted nothing more from him than some quick satisfaction. He should have felt thankful for her lack of interest in him as anything more than a lover.

And he did feel thankful. Sort of.

10

CLAIRE WOKE UP slowly, feeling oddly satisfied for reasons she couldn't pinpoint right away. The room was bright, as if sunlight had finally prevailed over the clouds, and a glimpse of the blue sky outside the window confirmed it—the storm had passed.

As the fog of sleep lifted from her brain, she remembered the night before. The frantic lovemaking, then the leisurely lovemaking that had turned into more leisurely lovemaking....

That's why she felt so satisfied.

She stretched and felt her hand and foot bump against something warm and hard. Mason, sleeping next to her, his bare back a smooth expanse that beckoned for a woman's touch. And then she noticed the fingernail marks—four on each side—she must have left during some wild moment of their night together.

With the potential for awkwardness or arguing so great, Claire decided she wasn't much interested in sticking around for morning-after pillow talk. Not that she minded a good argument under normal circumstances, but for some reason, with Mason, she didn't want to do it in the morning. As quietly as she could, she slipped out of bed, then gathered up her clothes and dressed.

She felt a little rude just leaving, so she wandered into the living room in search of pen and paper to leave a note. Having no luck, she tried the small kitchen and found what she needed next to the phone. But standing in what suddenly felt like an intimate part of Mason's suite, she found herself curious about him.

Did he cook or just order room service whenever he was home? What was it like living in a glorified hotel suite all the time, on one's own private island? Surely it occasionally drove a guy to break out the frying pan and scramble some eggs or something.

She peeked into his refrigerator and was surprised to see that it was fairly well stocked. Bottled water, beer, milk, orange juice, white wine, an array of condiments, a wheel of Brie… He probably paid someone to shop for him, and cook for him, too, for that matter.

She closed the fridge and checked inside a few cabinets, where she found more normal food. Some pretzels, canned soups, things you'd expect to find in someone's home.

And maybe that was part of Mason's problem. He made his home in hotel rooms.

One thing guys rarely guessed about Claire was that she loved to cook. They always labeled her as one of those helpless carryout chicks who was completely at a loss if faced with preparing any food more complicated than a microwave dinner. But rather the opposite was true. She'd been fascinated with cooking since her childhood, and although she didn't do it often living alone, she could whip up an impressive meal when she wanted to.

"We can order room service." Mason's voice startled her, and she swung around too fast, sending pen and paper flying out of her hand and onto the floor.

Claire didn't show off her cooking skills to just anyone. She much preferred surprising the select few guys who deserved her culinary attention with a lavish meal once they'd been dating for a while. And yet, for reasons she didn't care to analyze, she had a burning desire to cook for Mason.

Or maybe it was just that she was insanely hungry from having skipped dinner the night before.

"How about I make some omelets?"

He blinked, looking deliciously rumpled with his hair mussed, the start of a beard darkening his jaw and a pair of navy plaid pajama bottoms hanging low on his hips.

"You can cook?"

Claire shot him a look, almost ready to toss aside her Betty Crocker urges and just pick up the phone for room service. "I know a thing or two."

He rubbed a hand through his hair. "Be my guest then."

Fifteen minutes later, she'd whipped up two spinach-and-cheddar omelets and found an unopened bottle of champagne in the back of the fridge to make mimosas.

She arranged breakfast on a large coffee table in the middle of the living room, then went off in search of Mason. She found him in the bathroom shaving.

"Too bad," she said. "The five o'clock shadow was pretty hot."

He glanced over at her and smiled. "But you've got rug burn on your face."

For the first time, Claire noticed the raw sensation around her mouth. She looked in the mirror and saw the telltale red rash. "Oh well, that's what concealer is for. Breakfast is ready."

"Thanks. I'll be out in a sec."

Claire found one of Mason's sweatshirts and a pair of gym shorts in the dresser and took the liberty of changing out of the skimpy silver dress into them. They were big on her, but a heck of a lot more comfortable than her costume from the previous night. If it bothered him, he could remove them himself.

Back in the living room, she took a peek at his bookshelves. Mysteries, thrillers, classics, contemporary literature. She never would have guessed she and Mason shared the same taste in reading material—or that he was even a reader—but she spotted several of her favorite mystery authors in his collection.

A glance at his magazine rack revealed a more predictable stash of reading material—news and business magazines, plus a few guy magazines that seemed right up Mason's alley. She picked up the one on top, last month's copy of *Excess,* and sat down next to the coffee table to thumb through it.

The magazine focused on what was really important to men—women, expensive toys, fast cars and more women. An article about how to keep your girlfriend coming back for more caught Claire's attention, so she flipped back to it.

A couple of minutes later when Mason appeared at the table across from her, she looked up at him and smiled. "I can't believe you were making fun of my reading taste last night. I hope you don't follow the crappy dating advice they give in here."

He eyed the photo on an open page of a woman in a black lace bra and panties. "I just buy that magazine for the pictures," he said in a tone that made it impossible to tell if he was joking or serious. Since it was an echo of her own comment about *Chloe* magazine from the night before, she decided it was a joke.

"You read Elmore Leonard?" she asked, nodding at his bookshelves.

"Everything he's ever written."

Claire blinked. Finally, something they could agree upon. "He's brilliant, isn't he?"

"The best." He eyed the omelet. "Wow, you shouldn't have gone to all this trouble."

Claire picked up a fork and stabbed a bite from her plate. "No trouble. I don't tell this to guys I'm dating, but I actually attended culinary school for a short while."

"And you hide this from your dates because?"

She took a bite. Not her best work, but not bad for what she'd had to work with. "I know how men are. You find out a woman likes to cook and suddenly you expect her to do it every night."

He tasted the omelet and moaned in appreciation. "Wow, this is delicious."

"Thanks."

"Aren't you worried that you might actually impress me or something?"

Claire glanced down at the magazine that was still open on the table. "According to this magazine, all I need to do is stay awake and wear sexy underwear, and I can't help but impress you."

He smiled. "Probably true."

She flipped to another article, this one steamy fantasy letters from readers. "Listen to this," she said. "'How I made my flight attendant fantasy come true…'" She glanced up at Mason. "Do you have a flight attendant fantasy?"

"Depends on the flight attendant."

"I'll bet every guy does. Mile-high club and all."

He cocked an eyebrow. "Are you a member?"

"Are you?"

"I asked you first."

"Sadly, no. I think airplane bathrooms are just too disgusting to get romantic in."

"That's what chartered jets are for."

Claire laughed. "My travel agent discount doesn't cover chartered jets, unfortunately."

Mason was devouring his omelet like a starving man. When he finished it, he looked up and smiled. "You must like to travel, with your job."

"Some girls played house or Barbie dolls or school. I played airline stewardess and sailor."

Both eyebrows shot up this time. "Um, stewardess and sailor?"

Claire rolled her eyes. "Not at the same time! I mean, I played stewardess because I saw them on TV and wanted to wear the cool uniform, and other times I played sailor because I was a big Popeye fan and I loved the ocean."

"And, of course, both careers offer the opportunity for travel," he said smiling.

"Of course."

"I bet you were a spitfire as a little girl," he said, looking at her in a way that made her turn her attention to her omelet.

Claire poked at it, suddenly not so hungry. Okay, so she was a complete spaz when it came to intimate conversation. So she was afraid of letting her real feelings hang out in front of the wrong person.

Mason was definitely the wrong person.

"I was daddy's little princess, completely spoiled, always got whatever I wanted."

He nodded. "That explains a lot."

"Screw you." Claire immediately regretted mentioning her father. It was a subject she avoided with almost everyone.

"Sorry, I couldn't resist." He finished off his mimosa, then asked, "What about your Dad? Is he still around?"

"Actually, no. He passed away recently in a car accident." Claire willed her voice to remain casual, free of emotion, just the way she wanted to keep their conversation.

His expression darkened. "I'm sorry. That must have been really tough for you."

She shrugged. "That's life, right?"

"You don't have to act like this around me, you know. I expect you to have actual feelings about your family."

"Right."

"What about your mother? Does she live in Phoenix?"

"She died when I was ten. Breast cancer."

Mason frowned, silent for a few moments, while Claire struggled to recover the carefree feeling she'd had a few minutes ago.

"That must have made your father passing away even more difficult," he finally said.

She was such an idiot. Tears were welling up in

her eyes, and she was about to start bawling like a baby in front of the guy she was trying to screw out of her system.

"Are you okay?" He stood up and came over to her, sat down beside her and held her arm when she tried to scoot away.

She felt her lower lip quivering. She was the biggest idiot on earth. "Yes, of course I am."

"No you're not."

"I'm just losing my freaking mind, that's all." She was starting to blubber now, out of nowhere, like the soon-to-be mental patient she was.

Mason wrapped his arms around her and pulled her close, and she found herself resting her head on his shoulder, feeling a lot more comforted than she would have liked by his embrace.

She was taking whimpery little breaths now, like a toddler who'd missed nap time. Maybe she hadn't let herself mourn her father for as long as she'd needed to, but why it was all coming out now was beyond her.

After a few minutes, she'd calmed down, and she pulled away from Mason. "Sorry," she said, wiping at her eyes.

"It's okay. You're supposed to be upset about things like this."

"I'm not supposed to become a basket case over morning-after omelets." She stood up and cleared the plates off the coffee table.

"I'll get those," Mason protested, but she was already on the way to the kitchen.

"You get the glasses," she called over her shoulder.

Once she'd put the dishes in the sink, she turned to him. "I should go," she said. "You probably have work to do today, right?"

"Yeah, unfortunately I do have to go to the office for a while."

He pulled her to him and kissed her on the forehead. "Why don't you relax and enjoy your vacation today, and maybe we could meet up again tonight? Say around dinnertime?"

Claire couldn't help but smile at the thought of another night with Mason, doing more of what they'd already done. No, she definitely wasn't cured of him yet.

"Sounds good," she said. "How about you come get me around six?"

"Let's make it five-thirty so we'll have plenty of time for a little pre-dinner appetizer, if you know what I mean."

Did she ever. Claire sighed into Mason's chest, marveling at the roller coaster of emotions he managed to evoke in her. Anger, desire, giddiness, more desire, melancholy, excitement…

If they didn't work out a cure soon, she wasn't sure what she'd do with herself. Maybe find a nice white jacket and a quiet little room with padded walls, where she could go absolutely crazy without harming any bystanders.

MASON WAS PRETTY SURE e-mail would be the downfall of civilization. He felt like he spent more time reading and responding to it than doing anything else, and now that he'd wasted an entire morning answering business e-mail, he'd had enough.

The drudgery of it had been oddly soothing, the one thing that took his mind off of Claire. He'd spent the weekend holding her at arm's length emotionally as they stayed anything but arm's length in bed.

And having her break down in front of him over breakfast had thrown him for a loop. He'd ached for her, and he'd found himself wanting to see more of her inner landscape. What made Claire the woman she was fascinated him a hell of a lot more than he would have liked. It reminded him of why he liked to keep things simple, uncomplicated, easy.

A handful of a woman like Claire was anything but.

He gave himself a mental shake and forced his mind back on work.

Today his first order of business should have been firing Mike D'Amato and tracking down everyone involved in the whole dominatrix business. But he wasn't ready to deal with it yet. He wasn't mentally focused enough, and he needed someone to bounce ideas off. He was tempted to find Claire and use her as his sounding board, but he feared he'd lose all focus again if she were anywhere nearby.

He was just closing his e-mail program when the

reception desk buzzed him. Mason pressed the inter-com button. "Yeah?"

"Mr. Cayhill is here to see you."

"Send him back."

A few seconds later, there was a tap on the door. "Come on in."

Carter stepped inside and closed the door behind him. "Hey, you have time to look over the entertain-ment schedule for the next season with me?"

"Sure." Regardless of whatever else was going wrong at Escapade, at least Mason could always be assured the entertainment was taken care of. Carter had handled his job as entertainment director for the resort flawlessly from day one.

Carter sat down across from him. "You're look-ing a little stressed, man. What's going on?"

Was Claire really getting to him so much that cas-ual observers could tell he was losing his mind?

Mason shrugged. His first instinct was to tell Car-ter about his problem with Mike D'Amato, but then he heard himself blurt, "Woman trouble."

"Ah, that hot little redhead I saw you with over the weekend?"

Mason couldn't recall having seen Carter, but it was a small world at the resort, and it was hard to go more than a few days without spotting just about everyone he knew.

"She's a serious source of trouble."

Carter laughed. "Most of them are, you know."

"Actually, there's nothing serious going on there," Mason said, backtracking. He suddenly wasn't interested in discussing Claire with anyone. "The real problem is here at the resort. Maybe you could give me some advice."

"Sure, man. What's up?"

"Have you heard any wild rumors going around about dominatrix services for hire here at Escapade?"

Carter blinked, then after recovering from his speechless state, he laughed. "That's crazy."

"I got my information from a trustworthy source," Mason said.

He sobered. "Okay, I'll sniff around and see what I can turn up. It has to be an inside job, since we're the only ones living on the island full-time."

"Right. I'm just pissed off that my own employees would risk ruining the image of the resort this way." Mason hesitated, not sure if he should tell Carter everything he knew.

But if Carter was going to help rout out the problem employees, he'd need all the information he could get. "Listen," he said. "There's more. You familiar with Mike D'Amato, the bartender at the Cabana Club?"

"Sure, I know him."

"He appears to be running this thing. I've also got a physical description of a woman involved in it, but no name yet."

"So how do you want to handle them?"

"I'll let our security guys decide what to do with

Mike. He'll be fired, of course, but on top of that, I'm not sure what they might be able to do to get him to talk."

Carter shook his head. "Never surprises me the things people do. But don't you worry, because if anyone can get to the bottom of this, it's me. People trust me—they'll talk."

"Thanks, Carter. I really appreciate your help."

"Why don't you let me talk to Mike D'Amato before you fire him?"

"I don't know. I'm afraid he'll run if he figures out we're on to him."

"Hey, it's your call. If you give me the physical description of the other woman, I'll see what I can do to track her down."

"Security's on that, too. They've got a photo database of all the resort employees, so it's just a matter of time until they get a match."

"All right, man. Let me know if there's anything else I can do to help."

"I will, thanks."

Mason felt as if a weight had been lifted from his shoulders. With Carter keeping his ear to the ground, there wasn't any reason for him to dwell on the problem. People were handling it, and if there was one thing Mason knew was crucial to good management, it was delegating responsibility.

"You sure you feel like talking business right now?" Carter asked.

"Absolutely. What've you got for me?"

He listened as Carter went over the planned events for the next season and highlighted problem areas he was still working on. But Mason's mind wandered after a while, and he found himself thinking about Claire again.

About his comment to Carter—woman trouble.

No two words could have summed up Claire more succinctly, and yet, they nagged at him. Why had she been the first subject he blurted out, when he hadn't even wanted to talk about her?

Why was he letting her get under his skin? And if she did, then what?

Then she'd walk away, cured of her desire for his services in bed, and he'd be left here wanting more. Theirs was a no-win situation, and he'd be best off remembering that fact.

Claire was a temporary fling, nothing more.

By the time Carter was finishing up his report, Mason had become preoccupied with more than just his problems with Claire. His mind had wandered straight into the bedroom, where all his energy with her should have been focused. No more intimate conversation, if he could help it. He'd focus on the task at hand—curing Claire before all hell broke loose.

11

CLAIRE SPENT HER FIRST free day on the island trying to work out the tension in her shoulders. She'd gone to the spa for a massage, a manicure and a pedicure. She'd walked along the beach enjoying the sunshine—while trying to avoid the many single guys out looking for easy sex—and she'd read a paperback novel beside the pool.

But try as she might, she hadn't managed to put Mason out of her thoughts for more than a minute or two. And he was most definitely the source of all the tension in her shoulders.

She'd enjoyed herself partly because she liked traveling alone and partly because Escapade was a fabulous resort, but she couldn't kid herself. She'd been looking forward to tonight like crazy, hoping it would be the night that would finally do the trick—but mostly just looking forward to it.

A knock on the door alerted Claire to Mason's arrival. She did a quick check in the mirror, mussed her hair a bit, and adjusted her satin robe so that it gaped open ever-so-enticingly in the front.

There. Now he'd have no choice but to attack her at the door.

She'd already showered, put on her makeup and laid out an outfit for the evening, but first she'd made sure to be prepared for the pre-dinner appetizer he'd mentioned.

Mason was a little early, but that was okay.

She smiled as she opened the door, grasping the loosely tied belt of her robe and preparing to pull it free so that her robe would fall all the way open.

"I've been waiting—" The words died on her lips when she saw her best friend standing in the hallway, Mason nowhere in sight. "Lucy! What are you doing here?"

"I might ask you the same thing," Lucy said, blinking at Claire's barely dressed appearance so close to dinnertime.

Shock quickly gave way to giddiness at having such an unexpected pleasant surprise, and the two women embraced. Claire hadn't realized how much she'd missed Lucy until now. With no siblings of her own, and her parents gone, Lucy had become not just her best friend but also her family.

When they finished hugging, Claire tugged her robe closed tighter and stepped aside for her friend to come in, then shut the door behind her.

"You're supposed to be running the travel agency," Claire said, hoping to divert attention from her own questionable behavior.

Lucy raised one eyebrow and crossed her arms over her chest. "I left it in the capable hands of Gill."

"But, why are you here?"

"I've been telling Judd to bring me here since before the resort opened. When he wrapped up a case this weekend sooner than expected, and you made your little unexpected voyage here, I finally convinced him we needed to show up and support his brother's latest business venture."

"So you came to keep an eye on me?" Claire said, feeling oddly flattered at the notion.

"No, we came to have a much-needed vacation," she answered, then smiled sheepishly. "And to keep an eye on you."

"Well, I'm glad you're here, regardless."

"Tropical Storm Macy almost kept us away, but here we are. Now tell me who you were expecting to show up at your door dressed like this."

"Room service."

"Right."

"Where's Judd?" Claire asked.

"He's off looking for Mason."

"Does Mason know you're here?"

Lucy smiled, looking mischievous. "It's a surprise for him, too."

"You look great," Claire said. "Did you get highlights or something?"

Lucy's light brown hair sparked with silvery blond streaks that made her warm brown eyes look even warmer. Ever since she'd met Judd, she had the habit of looking ridiculously happy, but today, she was positively glowing.

She smiled and ran her fingers through her wavy shoulder-length hair. "I went to your stylist on Saturday. He did something amazing that cost way too much money, but you're changing the subject." She narrowed her eyes at Claire. "*Who* were you expecting at your door just now?"

"Are you sure that's all there is? Did you get some sun this weekend?"

"Would you stop with my appearance? I didn't get any sun, okay!"

"Okay, fine. I was expecting Mason. Does that make you happy?"

Lucy sighed, not looking nearly as smug as Claire had expected. "What's the deal with that dominatrix service you told me about?"

"Mason's investigating, and I'm helping. Sort of. I think we've found the guy who's orchestrating the thing, but so far no one is talking."

"Good thing Judd's here then. He'll get it all figured out, and that'll be one less thing Mason has to worry about."

"Is that how you really lured Judd here?"

"No, believe it or not. He wanted to come even before I told him about the service."

Claire thought of her and Mason's costumed foray into private investigating and laughed. "It's a good thing he's here, because Mason and I aren't exactly pros at this P.I. stuff."

Lucy smiled, oh-so-casually. "What's going on between you two?"

"Why don't you ask your brother-in-law that question?"

"Will his answer be different from yours?"

"Yes, because I'm not going to answer." Claire stalked over to the window and frowned at the sky, which had the nerve to be looking absolutely breathtaking at that moment, alight with the soft early evening glow that invited romantic strolls with lovers.

For some immature reason, she wasn't keen on having her actions over the weekend examined under Lucy's magnifying glass.

"You are such a liar," Lucy said, sitting down on Claire's bed, ever the patient friend. "You know you're dying to tell me every scandalous detail of your weekend with him."

Under normal circumstances, Lucy would have been right. Claire supposed she couldn't exactly tell her best friend nothing about the weekend.

"I guess things just got a little out of hand. I might be violating some kind of brother-in-law, sister-in-law bond if I tell you *everything*."

Lucy started looking a little queasy. "I don't *want* you to tell me *everything*. Just the important stuff."

Claire gave up and sat down beside her, reclining back on a pile of pillows. "Okay, important stuff to you means, am I in love? Have we set a wedding date yet? The answer to both those questions is no."

"I wouldn't expect anything more from you. I was hoping you'd say something like, 'We really like each other. We've finally stopped arguing long enough to see that we have a lot in common.'"

Claire started to protest, but then she realized Lucy was right. When they weren't arguing—and even when they were—she had fun with Mason.

Now what the hell was she supposed to do with that annoying little fact?

"I'll admit he's not the complete jerk-off I originally thought he was."

Lucy peered at her from the corner of her eye. "And?"

"And we may have experienced a few pleasant moments over the weekend."

"Pleasant enough that you might both have dinner at the same table as Judd and me tonight?"

Claire shrugged. Her plans for pre-dinner sex clearly weren't going to happen now. "Sure, I think we can sit through dinner together."

It would just give them the energy they needed to do what would happen later, when they finally got each other alone.

"Well, then I have instructions to hurry you down to the seafood restaurant near the resort entrance. We're supposed to meet Judd there in twenty minutes."

Claire got dressed while Lucy filled her in more

on how she'd managed to convince Judd that they needed to take a vacation on such short notice, but Lucy was a notoriously bad liar. There was some important fact she was leaving out of the story.

Claire turned and watched Lucy as she paced impatiently around the room. It wasn't like Lucy to pace impatiently or talk a mile a minute. Something about her had changed, that was for sure, and Claire couldn't begin to name what it was.

MASON HAD WATCHED Judd and Lucy exchange knowing glances all through dinner, so when they both announced at the same moment, "We have some news to tell you," it didn't exactly come as a surprise.

Claire looked up from her bananas Foster. "What kind of news?"

"We're pregnant!" Lucy said, beaming.

Claire froze with a spoonful of banana and ice cream hovering inches from her mouth, her eyes wide. "Pregnant?"

"Yes! It's a little sooner than we expected, but we're so excited, we thought we'd fly out here to tell you both at the same time."

"Congratulations!" Mason stood up and hugged Lucy, then Judd, and sat back down as he let the news settle in his brain. He was happy for them, and he loved the idea of having a kid in the family. But…

But what?

He was also suddenly feeling a little off. Like he'd

eaten some bad seafood. And then he realized what was bugging him. If his little brother had kids first— just as he'd gotten married first—and if Mason continued on his current path toward eternal bachelorhood, he'd eventually become one of those eccentric old guys who never married and never had kids.

That fact hadn't really bothered him when it was just the opinions of his peers he had to consider, many of whom were still swinging singles. But now there'd be a kid in the family, possibly more than one. And when viewed through the eyes of a child, his eternal bachelorhood could seem...well, odd.

He'd be *Weird Old Uncle Mason.*

He wasn't sure that's who he wanted to be.

"Mason? Are you okay?" Lucy asked.

He snapped out of his daze. Claire had gotten up to hug Judd and Lucy too and was offering them her congratulations.

"I'm fine, really. I guess I'm just getting sentimental over my little brother having a baby. Have you told Mom yet?"

"I'm not even sure where she is right now," Judd said. "Pakistan?"

Mason shook his head. "I got an e-mail from her last week. She's in Bali."

After their parents' divorce, they'd had occasional awkward visits with their father that had eventually ended when he married again and started a second family. Neither of them had heard from him in nearly fifteen years, so that left their mom as the person to tell about major life events like a baby.

That is, if she were ever around to hear the news. She'd spent her retirement years globetrotting, and her distance was part of what had kept Judd and Mason close. They stuck together through everything, and Mason realized with a start that he wanted to be around to watch Judd's kid grow up.

Which would mean living in Arizona.

Near Claire.

The bad-seafood feeling came back with a vengeance.

Judd, Lucy and Claire were discussing due dates and baby names and such, so they didn't notice what must have been the shade of green Mason was turning. He decided if he didn't want to seem like a complete jerk, he needed to snap out of his funk and get into the baby talk.

"If it's a boy," he joked, "I'll cast my vote for the name Mason—strong, distinctive, simple—"

"Actually, Lucy already suggested that," Judd said, much to Mason's surprise. "I told her it would give you too much of a big head."

If Mason wasn't mistaken, he would have sworn Claire was working just as hard as he was to disguise a queasy feeling over the whole notion of parenthood. He watched her as she neglected the dessert she'd been attacking only minutes ago. After their dessert plates were cleared away, he was sure he saw relief on her face when Lucy said she was tired and wanted to go back to their room to get some rest.

"I'll see you in the morning then," Claire said, standing up from the table a little quicker than everyone else.

They said their goodbyes to Judd and Lucy and found themselves alone on Escapade's main promenade that led down to the beach. It was dark out now, but the resort's walkways were lit, and the sound of the ocean beckoned.

A few hours ago, he'd had little on his mind but getting Claire alone in her room, but now… A walk seemed more appropriate given his weak stomach.

"Want to go for a stroll on the beach?" he asked as Claire brushed a wild curl out of her eyes.

"I'd love to." She was wearing a slinky white dress with a sweater draped over her shoulders, so he took the liberty of removing it and helping her into it.

After a few minutes of walking, he said, "You seemed a little shocked by the baby news."

"I wasn't the one turning green."

Mason laughed. "I'm actually thrilled for them. I don't know why the news threw me so off-kilter."

"I'm thrilled for them, too." She looked down at the sand and hugged her arms around herself as she walked. "I guess it's just that when you're our age and someone you're close to has a kid, then it makes you think, you know?"

"Believe me, I know."

Mason knew better than to have the kid conversation with a woman he wasn't planning to marry, but he and Claire were so far from being an actual dating couple that he felt safe asking, "You want to have kids someday?"

She shrugged. "I'm not opposed to the idea of procreation. I guess I've always assumed I would someday when I'm too old to worry about stretch marks."

"Which will be when? When you're eighty?"

"Something like that."

She smiled, and he found a whole new reason to like her. She could talk about kids without getting that glazed, desperate, my-clock-is-ticking look so many women got.

"How about you? Any paternal urges?"

"I'm pretty much with you on the whole parenthood issue, except for the part about stretch marks, of course. I've always considered it one of those events that would happen in the unforeseeable future."

"Do men get stretch marks?" Claire asked, giving him an easy out.

He should have felt relieved. Instead, he sort of wished they could keep going with the soul-baring conversation. But this was Claire, after all. Claire, who'd leave as soon as she'd gotten her fill of him. There was no sense in getting too friendly.

"I don't know, but you're welcome to search me later."

She laughed. "I can say with confidence that you

do not have a single stretch mark. Not that I've been looking for them, but I would have noticed something like that."

· They continued up the beach in the direction of Mason's suite, and he was happy to realize his bad-seafood feeling had disappeared. He was starting to enjoy Claire's company out of bed just as much as he enjoyed it in bed, and that was an interesting development.

Interesting, but probably not important.

"LITTLE BROTHER, I'M DAMN glad you're here," Mason said as he leaned against his desk.

Judd sat in Mason's office chair, staring at the computer as he scrolled through employee files, looking for anything fishy to narrow down their pool of dominatrix suspects.

"Has resort security come up with any leads on who's working for this Mike D. guy?"

"A few employees with criminal records as of this morning, but nothing solid."

"I promised Lucy I wouldn't spend our whole vacation working on this, but I do want to help you. Can you schedule a meeting between me and your security guys, so we can share information?"

"Definitely. If you talk to my assistant on the way out, she'll call them and get you set up."

"I've spotted a couple of former strippers on your payroll. That's one place to look further. If they're willing to take their clothes off for cash, then maybe they're willing to go a step further."

"Good thought."

Judd sat back in the leather chair and crossed his arms over his chest. "Who on your management team do you trust, and who don't you trust?"

Mason frowned at the question. "I can't say I completely trust anyone. The resort's only been open two months, so I don't know anyone that well yet."

"Anyone you definitely don't trust?"

"No, can't say there is. Why would you look at management first?"

"It takes some kind of management skill to organize an underground ring of any illegal activity and have it be successful. Maybe Mike D'Amato was just the front man, and someone else was or is running the show."

"Who says they're successful?"

"We don't know. I'm just guessing here," Judd said, turning his attention back to the employee database.

"I think I've got a solid management team, but I've been wrong before."

"You have any disgruntled ex-girlfriends here on the island?" Judd said.

"You think you're funny, don't you?"

"I'm dead serious. The way you piss off women..."

"I haven't pissed off a single woman since Natasha," Mason said, referring to his ex who'd tried to ruin the Fantasy Ranch.

Judd looked at him, one eyebrow raised.

"Okay, not counting Claire."

"Claire counts."

"She's not a girlfriend."

Or was she?

"Then what exactly would you call her?"

A pain in the ass, was his first thought.

"I don't know," he finally said.

And that was the truth. He had no idea what label to put on Claire, no inkling what she meant in his life, no way to measure the hurricane-like impact she had on him.

She was just Claire. Completely indefinable.

"I'd call her the woman who's going to haunt you the rest of your life if you don't get serious and make peace with her."

"I've made about as much peace with her as any one man can make."

"Peace and sex are not the same thing," Judd said.

His little brother knew him too damn well.

"Who says I ever have to get serious about any woman? I'm doing just fine as is. No need to mess with perfection."

"You call this perfection? Living on a little island where your only relationship possibilities are either the one-week variety or the kind that involve screwing people who work for you?"

"The one-week variety is my favorite kind, and I consider employees off-limits."

Judd held up his hand in defeat. "Fine, if you want to keep on kidding yourself…"

"So now you're going to be a father, and you have to start acting like my dad, too?"

He grinned. "Looks that way."

"Don't think you're getting out of being the little brother that easily. I can still kick your ass."

"Let me see you try it."

Mason gave Judd a playful smack on the side of the head. A second later, Judd was up out of the chair, his head butting into Mason's stomach. He toppled him onto the ground and then put him in a headlock.

They wrestled around on the floor beside the desk, alternately laughing and muttering curses, neither of them stronger than the other. For a few minutes, Mason could imagine they were still kids, without a care in the world other than beating the other's ass.

"Okay, damn it. You win," he finally said.

"You're still a wuss." Judd stood up and offered Mason a hand.

"And you're still a big pussy."

"I might be a pussy, but at least I know my boys can swim."

Mason laughed. He may not have had any strong paternal urges, but there was that ever-present male desire to know for sure that he could father a child if he wanted to. "You got me there, man."

"But seriously, I have to tell you, I want you to be the baby's godparent. Lucy and I both do."

He blinked at the sudden serious turn the conversation had taken. Not what he'd expected, and it nearly knocked him down with its gravity. "Whoa. You sure about that? I mean, I don't know anything about kids or being a godparent."

Judd clapped him on the shoulder. "You'll learn, bro."

"Well, if you're sure…"

"I wish you'd move back to Arizona, you know. I miss playing ball with you, and I want you around to teach the kid to play."

Mason swallowed a lump in his throat. "I'll probably be spending more time in Arizona again soon, once I've got Escapade running the way I want it."

"I'll believe it when I see it."

"Hey man, you've helped me enough today. You'd better go spend some time with that wife of yours."

Judd glanced at his watch. "You're right. I told her I'd be back to go to the beach with her by now."

"I'll catch up with you later."

Mason watched as Judd left the office, closing the door behind him. Alone again, a vague feeling of discontent settled in his belly. Discontent that his brother was suddenly trying to sell him on Claire and on the whole convention of settling down.

And discontent that for once, Judd's argument wasn't sounding so crazy.

12

CLAIRE HAD BEEN AT Escapade for five days, and still she wasn't ready to leave. She'd spent every night with Mason, trying her damnedest to get her fill of Mason—trying to prove to herself that she absolutely was not a victim to his charms—and she was finally starting to admit to herself that maybe her plan just wasn't going to work.

Now that Judd and Lucy were there, too, she had company during the day most of the time, so it shouldn't have been too hard to get her mind off of Mason. But it was. When she wasn't with him, she was thinking about him, and when she was with him, she was thinking about him.

She was beginning to think psychotherapy might be the next logical step.

Now she was at one of the resort's bars with Judd and Lucy, while Mason was at some sort of business-related meeting. He'd told her the day before that the whole dominatrix problem had been dealt with, and he'd thanked her for her help. Maybe that had been his subtle way of letting her know she could leave any time now, but her body wasn't taking the hint.

"So," Lucy was saying to her, "are you and Mason having dinner together with us again tonight?"

"You two have got to stop it," Claire said, feeling like a zoo animal under Judd and Lucy's scrutiny.

"What?" Judd asked, suddenly Mr. Innocent.

"The matchmaking! Mason and I are not going to get together, so just give it up."

Judd smiled. "Let me just say for the record that I have been completely opposed to any and all matchmaking efforts from the start and have not willingly or knowingly participated in said efforts."

"Right."

Lucy took a sip of her virgin piña colada, pretending not to hear the conversation.

"Lucy, tell her!"

She peered over the rim of her glass—another bad actor at work. After taking another drink, she set the glass down. "Not that I'm admitting to any matchmaking efforts myself, but I can say with certainty that Judd has not willingly participated in any such thing."

"You two are impossible." Claire propped her elbows on the bar, looking across at the patrons on the other side. A scattered group of men and women chatted, laughed and drank. Claire should have felt happy and energized. Here she was at a beautiful resort with two of her favorite people in the world, yet she felt anything but carefree.

"Excuse me, but I need to take a walk to the ladies' room. Claire?"

"I'm fine, thanks."

Lucy disappeared, and Judd tipped his beer to Claire. "She means well," he said, "but she's not gonna rest until you and Mason either kill each other or get married."

"That's what I was afraid of."

"She thinks of it as her debt to you for introducing us."

Claire couldn't help smiling. She'd never imagined how sending Lucy on that birthday trip to the Fantasy Ranch would transform her best friend's life so completely. Not only had Lucy managed to fall in love with and marry the guy who was supposed to be her no-strings-attached fling, but she'd found a level of confidence in herself that she'd lacked before.

"She should consider her debt paid in full."

Judd gave her a look that said "not a chance," and Claire knew he was right. Lucy could be the most hardheaded person on earth when she thought she was right.

A guy who'd clearly been hitting the free froufrou drinks at the pool at little too hard came wandering in and weaved his way over to the empty bar stool next to Judd. Claire could smell the rum on him from three bar stools away.

He waved down the bartender and ordered a

whiskey sour, then propped himself on the bar and smiled at Judd. "You staying here long?"

"For about a week," Judd answered.

"Shingle guy like you," he slurred, "there's a lot of fun to be had, lemme tell you."

Judd opened his mouth, probably to protest his single status, but Drunken Guy continued.

"I know whatcher thinkin'. You've already heard the official spiel on the resort."

"Yeah," Judd said, "my brother's the—"

"But lemme tell you what you may not know." He leaned in close and attempted to whisper. "Anything you want, you can buy it here—companionship of whatever kind you like, if you catch my drift."

Claire could still hear him, though he clearly thought he and Judd were having a private one-on-one conversation. She focused her eyes on her drink and pretended to be oblivious to them.

She could almost see Judd's private-investigator antennae on alert now. "Oh yeah? Like what?"

Drunken Guy made a sweeping gesture. "Anything. Just last night…" He paused and waggled his eyebrows. "I had two girls come to my room for two hours of working me over like you wouldn't believe."

She didn't dare look over to see Judd's expression. After a moment, he asked, "Really? How much did it cost you?"

"Eh, about a grand. I own a sewage-treatment

plant outside of Toledo. Cost don't matter to me, and lemme tell you, it was worth every damn penny."

"So how do I hook up with these ladies?" Judd asked.

Drunken Guy fumbled in his wallet and pulled out a business card. "Drop me a line if you ever need help with sewage treatment."

He flipped the card over and grabbed a pen from nearby on the bar, then started scrawling a number on the card. "What you do is you call this number and just say you've got cash to burn."

"And they'll know what I want."

"You name it, and they'll get it for you for the right price. Until a few days ago you just had to talk to a guy at the Cabana Club, but he disappeared, so now it's a little more complicated."

"As in?"

"You just gotta make the phone call, then somebody calls you back, finds out what you want and tells you where to bring the money."

Judd took the card from him. "This person got a name?"

"Nah. It's all hush-hush."

"Thanks, man. Me and my wife might be into some fun, you know?"

Drunken Guy noticed Judd's wedding ring for the first time. "Oh, right. Hey man, whatever floats your boat."

He turned his attention to his drink just as Lucy

reappeared from the restroom. "Hey sweetheart," Judd said a little too enthusiastically. "Why don't we get going now?"

Claire looked over to see Judd giving Lucy a meaningful look. Lucy stared at him perplexed, but said nothing. After putting some money on the bar to cover their drinks, Judd and Lucy left, and Claire waited a minute before following. She found them outside waiting for her.

"What was up with that?" she said to Judd.

Judd frowned. "Looks like Mason's still got some problems to deal with."

Judd and Lucy had been filled in on the whole dominatrix-for-hire situation, but Mason had been confident that the perpetrators had been dealt with and that anyone else involved would be too afraid of getting caught to continue.

"I can't believe this stuff is still going on," Lucy said as they started walking back toward their hotel rooms.

"Sounds like it's not strictly S and M so much as it is a whole prostitution ring," Claire said, feeling sick for Mason. He'd been working nonstop to keep the resort running smoothly, and now this.

"We need to gather all the facts before we go to Mason," Judd said. "He's busy enough without having to deal with this again, too."

There were definitely some perks to having a private investigator for a brother, Claire supposed, not the least of which was having someone who could do the investigating when an illegal prostitution ring popped up on one's private island.

"So," Claire said, remembering their plans for the evening. "Are we still going to that 'Come As Who You Really Are' party? It starts in an hour."

"*This* is who I really am," Lucy said, gesturing to her pink top and khaki shorts. "It's a pretty boring costume."

"I think we can come up with something more interesting than that," Claire said, remembering the backstage costume area at the theater. She was pretty sure Mason wouldn't mind if they borrowed a few things again.

Judd sighed. "Lucy made me pack my cowboy boots and my Stetson, so I guess that'll be my costume."

"And jeans! He'll definitely be wearing jeans, too." Lucy smiled, and Claire knew she was remembering the way they'd first met, with Judd in that very same outfit, handcuffed to Lucy's bed. They'd been complete strangers, and Judd had been Claire's surprise birthday gift to Lucy.

Claire grabbed Lucy's hand. "Then you're coming with me. I know just the place to find an outfit that expresses the real you."

"But—"

"No arguing. You can't go to the party dressed like that." She nodded at a carry-on luggage bag sitting at the foot of the bed. "Is that empty?"

"Yes, why?"

"Bring it. We'll need it to carry the costumes."

"We'll meet you back at our room in a half hour," Lucy called to Judd as they took off, and ten minutes later, they were sneaking through the theater and into the costume area.

Thankfully, the janitor was nowhere in sight.

"How do you know about this place?" Lucy asked when Claire switched on the lights.

"Um, Mason showed it to me," she said, trying hard to keep a straight face.

"Why do I get the feeling there's a story behind that statement."

"Trust me when I say it's a story that would violate your brother-in-law, sister-in-law bond."

"Ooo-kaaaay," Lucy said, turning her attention to the rack of women's costumes.

"I'm thinking Las Vegas showgirls," Claire said, zeroing in on the costume Mason had liked so well before.

She smiled as she pictured what his reaction would be. That is, if he even got out of his meeting in time to make the party. They'd arranged to meet there as soon as he could break free, but he couldn't make any guarantees. Claire, for one, was dying to see the costume Mason considered a reflection of his true self.

"Claire, I am *so* not a showgirl."

"Then how about this?" Claire pulled out a scarlet dress of the sort worn by prostitutes of the Old West. "It'll match Judd's outfit."

Lucy's eyes lit up. "Perfect! I'm a harlot."

They tried on the costumes in their respective sizes, made a few adjustments to Lucy's with safety pins they found in a drawer, and then decided to just stay in costume until the party. After stuffing their street clothes into the carry-on bag, they left the costume area decked out in their new looks.

Claire was no stranger to turning heads, but even she felt a little silly at some of the stares they got on their way back. They were passing through a hallway adjoining theirs when a door swung open and the sounds of a party within came pouring out, along with a guy wearing a giant condom as a hat on his head.

"Hey, aren't you the girls we hired for the bachelor party? We've been waiting for you two."

Lucy started to protest, but Claire silenced her with a sharp elbow to the ribs.

"Um," Claire said, scrambling to decide how best to handle this. Clearly, this was a chance to find out more about the prostitution ring, and she didn't want to blow it. "Yep, that's us. Sorry if we're a little late."

"You're dressed kind of funny for a lesbian sex show," the guy said, frowning at their mismatched costumes.

"Oh, well, um, we actually were just told to dress up. I didn't realize we'd be doing a special show."

"Yeah, babe. Hope you came prepared with the dildos or whatever equipment you need."

Lucy made a strange noise, and Claire elbowed her again.

"Sure thing." She held up the carry-on bag as if it were full of sex equipment. "Just give us a second out here. We'll need to plan out our act a little bit before we get started."

"All right, but you better hurry. The guys are gettin' impatient in there." He stepped back inside and closed the door.

"What are you doing!" Lucy snapped.

"Don't you see, those guys hired prostitutes! This is our chance to get information for Judd's investigation."

"We're not really going in there."

Claire sighed. "I don't expect you to, but I am. I just want to poke around and see if I can get any information, maybe find out who they hired the prostitutes through."

"And then what? We have lesbian sex in front of a room full of drunken guys? Have you lost your mind?"

"No! We just make up some excuse and get out before anything happens." Then Claire saw the perfect plan laid out before her. "I've got it! You go on back to your room, and I'll go in and tell them my partner backed out at the last second, so no show."

"You can't go in there alone!"

"It's perfect. Don't worry about me. Besides, Judd would kill me if he found out I let you go in there."

Lucy crossed her arms over her chest. "I'm not letting you go in alone. I'm going, too."

Damn it.

But honestly, she was a little scared to go into a room full of drunken men alone, dressed like a show-girl. Maybe Lucy was right. They needed to find an alternative. "Okay, then here's the deal. We'll stall here in the hallway, make up some excuse about needing more equipment before we do the show and try to get some information from them."

Lucy frowned. "I like that better."

"I'll do all the talking, and you just try to stay quiet and follow my lead. Got it?"

"What if we get into trouble?"

"I've got my cell phone. We can call resort security if things get out of hand."

"Okay, you're right. I'm just overreacting, but if I have to feel you up or something, I'll never forgive you."

"You are *not* going to feel me up. We'll just make excuses and leave once we have our information."

Lucy tugged at her décolletage, making a disgruntled face as she did so.

"Okay, so tell me what I'm supposed to say again."

"You stay quiet, but if anyone asks, your name is Desiree and you only like girls."

Claire stopped as she was about to knock on the door. "Are you sure you want to do this, Luc? You can back out now if you want, and I'll just talk to them real quick myself."

"I'm not leaving you alone!" Lucy's brow scrunched up in her worried-friend look. "You're not getting scared, are you?"

Claire rolled her eyes and feigned confidence. "Of course not. I just don't want you to flub this."

She was an awful, horrid person, not even remotely deserving of a friend like Lucy, and she made a mental note to buy her a decadent gift as soon as they got off this stinking island.

Claire knocked on the door and a few seconds later, the condom-headed guy jerked it open.

"Let's get this show started," he said.

Behind him, Claire could see the bachelor party in progress. It reminded her of a scene from an eighties party, complete with half-naked women and more guys wearing giant condoms on their heads. That had to be some kind of safety hazard.

Could all these women be prostitutes? Surely not this many on Mason's private island. Probably they were just guests who felt comfortable wearing almost nothing in a room full of strangers.

It occurred to Claire that she was supposed to be taking charge, not gawking.

"We need payment first," she said.

The guy's expression transformed from ogling to pissed in an instant. "We already paid the money. Didn't he tell you that?"

"Which 'he' are you talking about?"

"You know who I mean—the guy on the phone."

"How'd you pay him, if you only talked to him on the phone?" Claire asked, going out on a shaky limb and praying it wouldn't backfire on her.

"Look, babe. I don't know what's going on here, but you've already gotten paid, so you better get in here and get the show rolling."

Claire produced a put-upon sigh. "Okay, we've got some kind of mix-up here. You tell me the name of the person you gave the money to, and I'll talk to them, then come back and do the show. How's that?"

"Look," the condom-head guy said, "this is my best friend's bachelor party. He's getting married tomorrow, and if he doesn't see two lesbians getting it on tonight, I'm gonna be seriously pissed."

What a loser, it took all Claire's willpower not to point out.

Lucy shot her a stricken look, and Claire raised her eyebrows in a silent plea for her to go along.

This was not playing out like she'd hoped.

"You'll have to take this up with our boss. We always collect the money up front before an act." Claire started edging away from the door, with Lucy right beside her.

"This is messed up!"

Nearby partiers had taken notice of the argument now and were stopping their conversations to watch and listen. Luckily, the blaring David Lee Roth rendition of "Just a Gigolo" made it impossible for people more than a few feet away to hear them.

"There's no need to get pissy," Claire said, careful to keep her voice free of the annoyance she felt. "I'll just go talk to—"

"This is some kind of scam, isn't it? You want me to pay you up front, and then you end up with twice the cash. You probably thought I'd be so drunk I wouldn't know the difference, huh?"

Claire took another step back. "Look, I don't tolerate belligerence. I don't care if you did pay. I'm not performing here with the way you're treating us." She looked at Lucy. "Let's get out of here."

"No way!" He stepped out into the hallway. "You're not going anywhere until we see some lesbian sex. Got it?"

Next to him, Lucy's expression turned to pure panic.

Claire smiled sweetly, leaned in close, and said, "Go screw yourself," at the same time that she jammed her heel into the guy's toe.

He howled at the pain, doubling over as he reached for his assaulted foot. "You bitch!"

Claire gave him a shove, and he stumbled backward as Lucy grabbed her wrist and started tugging on her to leave.

"Hey, what's going on over here?" a guy carrying a beer bottle asked as he caught his friend by the arm to keep him from falling.

Lucy pulled her down the hallway, and they ran out the main entrance of the building with the sound of the party still filtering out from the suite. Right outside the door, they passed by two women clad in black latex who looked like they really were on their way to perform a lesbian sex show.

Lucy and Claire gave each other knowing looks. Outside, resort guests were milling about, so they did a fast walk through the crowd and headed for the rear of the building.

"I'll call security and tell them to check out what's going on in that room," Claire said, pulling her cell phone out of her pocket.

"That was a close call," Lucy said, still breathless.

Claire was a little dizzy with adrenaline. She'd never meant to put her pregnant best friend in such a precarious situation. The stunt had been beyond stupid. "Yeah, close call."

She dialed the resort security number she'd seen printed on her Escapade information packet, and told them what she suspected was happening in the suite they'd just left, then hung up the phone.

"I think you could have kicked that guy's butt," Lucy said, smiling.

"He didn't stand a chance," she said, trying hard to sound lighthearted. What she'd done had been stupid, stupid, stupid, and she hadn't even learned anything helpful from it.

"I was so scared I almost peed on my harlot dress," Lucy said as they stopped in front of the hotel building entrance.

An uncontrollable bubble of stress-induced laughter forced itself up. "Me, too," Claire said between giggles.

"Are you coming up to our room?" Lucy asked.

"No, I want to find Mason now, tell him what we saw today."

"But—"

"I may not make it to the party," Claire said. "I'm feeling a little partied out after that whole scene."

"Me, too." Lucy gave her a funny look. "If I didn't know better, I might think you were actually smitten with Mason."

Smitten? Ridiculous.

"But you do know better, so don't even suggest it."

Claire could bluff all she wanted, but unfortunately, Lucy was pretty astute at reading her emotions. She made the mistake of looking away too soon, and Lucy was on to her.

"You *are* smitten!"

"It's a sex thing, Luc. There's a difference."

"You keep saying that. I think you're just trying to convince yourself that it's true," she said as she opened the door.

Sometimes, having such an astute best friend was a real pain in the ass.

13

MASON TOOK IN THE SIGHT of Claire—her breasts spilling out a red-sequined bra, her waist bare and her hips and thighs hardly covered by a matching fringed skirt—and his body temperature rose.

"Nice costume," he said. "I thought we were supposed to meet at the party."

He'd gotten out of his meeting earlier than expected and had just finished putting on his own costume when he'd heard the knock at the door.

"I changed my mind. It's been kind of a crazy afternoon and I was hoping you wouldn't mind skipping the party."

He stepped aside and let her in, then closed the door. "Crazy for you must be pretty crazy."

She filled him in on the drunken guest at the bar, then the impromptu crashing of the bachelor party, and he clenched his teeth to keep from spewing profanity.

"Tell me you're joking, that you didn't actually go to the door of a party full of drunken men dressed like this and posing as a prostitute."

She looked sheepish, possibly a first for Claire. "I could tell you that, but I'd be lying."

"Claire!"

"No one feels dumber than I do right now, okay?"

"Lucy was in on this, too? I thought at least one of you had some common sense."

"Nothing happened, we're both fine and I'd really appreciate it if you could stop with the guilt trip. Besides, one good thing came out of it—your security guys probably busted two of the dominatrixes."

Mason wanted to grab her and squeeze her, hold her close and never let her walk out the door again. Where had this insane protective urge come from? Claire was a grown woman, not one who needed his protection—but if that were true, she wouldn't have been pulling such stupid stunts.

So he did.

He caught her in his arms and pulled her to him. He'd seen her in plenty of bad-girl outfits, and this one was no more or less sexy than the rest, but something else entirely had him wanting to hold her close. He got a little tight in the throat just imagining her in danger.

"Wait." She tried to pull away from him, but he locked his arms around her waist and held her against him. "Thank you for going to all this trouble for me. I wish you hadn't done it, but I appreciate it."

"Playing the overprotective type doesn't suit you, Mason."

"I'm not being overprotective, I'm being sensible."

"A sensible pirate, hmm?" she said, finally commenting on his costume.

"Guess I got all dressed up for nothing if we're skipping the party."

"No, definitely not for nothing," she said, looking him over.

"You like pirates?"

"Mmm, hmm. I've always wanted to be ravaged by a dastardly pirate."

Mason felt himself stir. It never failed to surprise him how fast Claire could turn him on.

"That outfit looks pretty uncomfortable. Why don't you take it off?"

"How will I get back to my room if I'm not wearing any clothes?" She batted her eyelashes, a complete failure at looking innocent.

"I don't intend to let you leave here once you have your clothes off."

Her eyes darted to his lips, and when she met his gaze again, she was all mischief. "I think you must have me confused with a girl who's easy."

He dipped his head and tasted the satin flesh of her earlobe, then whispered into her ear, "The last word I'd use to describe you is easy."

She laughed and attempted to wriggle out of his grasp. "I'm warning you—you'd better let go of me or you'll regret it."

"Go ahead, give me your best shot," he said as he

caught her from behind in his arms, trapping her arms at her sides.

Claire did her best to jab him with an elbow or kick him with her heels, and Mason was surprised at her strength. When she managed to stomp his foot, he lifted her up from the ground and carried her to the couch, where he dropped her and climbed on top before she could kick him anywhere more painful.

"You are the most troublesome woman I've ever met."

She smiled. "I bet you can't wait until I leave Escapade."

He ignored the pang in his belly. It was true—part of him couldn't wait for her to leave. And another treacherous part of him couldn't imagine not having Claire around to make him crazy and arouse him like no other woman could.

"You're not going anywhere until you give me what I want."

She stopped struggling, went completely still. "Which is what?"

"To get you naked and have my way with you."

"Only if you promise to cure me of my problem tonight."

"I don't think there's a cure for being a pain in the ass," he said, and she clocked him on the side of the head.

"I mean, I need you all the way out of my system

before I can leave. So this is it, give it all you've got, and you'll be rid of me for good."

"Is that a threat or a promise?" Mason blurted before he could stop to consider what he meant.

"It's a dare," Claire said, her expression inscrutable.

He silenced her with one hungry kiss, and then another and another. She felt so alive, so hot, so perfect beneath him, he couldn't imagine not having her there.

What if this *was* their last night together? What if he would have this night burned in his memory forever as the last time he made love to Claire? Didn't he want to put an end to their constant tug-of-war? It was hard to imagine why when she slid her hands down his back and gripped his ass, pushed his hips into her as she ground against him.

This was so much more than sexual attraction. This, this, this *thing* between him and Claire—it was out of control.

He stopped, stilled himself on top of her, unsure what to do with his realization.

"You don't want to make me mad," Claire whispered. "I have a weapon and I know how to use it."

"What weapon?"

"Sex," she whispered.

"Mm. You're right, you do know how to use it."

Claire pushed against his chest until he sat up, and then she climbed on top of his lap and began unfastening his pants.

"Did I ever show that trick I learned from my roommate in college?"

"Your roommate?"

"Off campus. His name was Phil, and he gave legendary blow jobs."

Mason stared at her, speechless.

"Not to me, obviously. But he showed me his secrets."

She slid off the couch and between his legs, then freed his erection from his pants and held it in her palm. Mason watched as she dipped her head down, her crimson hair spilling across his belly, and he expelled an involuntary moan when she took him into her mouth.

This. This was what he would miss.

Not Claire herself, right?

No, it was the way she had with his body. The way she took charge, laid claim to him and acted completely without inhibition.

She ran her tongue along the ridge of his cock, then pulled back and let her breath cool him as she stroked his balls. He felt himself tighten, grow more and more ready, as he built up to the inevitable.

When she took him into her mouth again, she worked some magic with her teeth that had him straining against her, every muscle of his body coiled, ready to spring into action at the slightest invitation. She increased her pace, sucking, massaging, teasing and then satisfying, pushing him closer to the edge.

But one thought kept occurring to him through the haze of his pleasure: Claire was so much more than he'd expected, so much more interesting than he'd imagined, so much harder to let go of than he'd thought she would be…. What the hell was he supposed to do now?

She quickened her pace more, clearing his mind of all coherent thought, and he buried his fingers in her hair. "Claire," he gasped. "Don't stop."

And then she did just that. Just as he was about to spill himself into her mouth, she pulled away, pressed her fingertips strategically against his cock, and prolonged the crazy-sweet sensation of his near-climax.

"You want more?" she asked.

He was both tensed and limp, powerless and ready to spring up and pin her to the floor, push himself into her and properly finish what she'd started.

"You know I do," he said, his voice strained.

She smiled sweetly. "Then you'll have to come and take what you want, dastardly pirate."

There was just too much to love about this wild redhead, he thought, as he stood up and stripped off his clothes, his gaze pinned on her.

She simply sat back on the floor, her legs crossed as demurely as possible in the fringed skirt, her sweet ass peeking out the bottom of it.

Too much to love.

"For a woman as ballsy as you, you sure are acting suspiciously passive."

She batted her eyelashes. "Can't a girl get a little domination when she needs it?"

Mason found a condom in his wallet and put it on, then dropped to his knees and pushed Claire onto her back. "Lose the clothes and leave the sexy heels on," he said.

He watched her, riveted as she slowly took off her bra and let it slide down her arms until it hit the floor. Her breasts were lush and full, always managing to surprise him with their voluptuousness. Her expression full of mischief, she wriggled out of her skirt and panties, then reclined back on her elbows, wearing nothing but her shoes and a smile.

"Woman, you drive me wild," he said as he climbed on top of her and pushed her against the ground.

His erection was poised to pierce her where she was the most hot and wet, nearly making him dizzy with desire.

"You want to punish me?"

"If you call this punishment," he said as he pushed inside her.

All the way, he filled her up. Watched her face transform from mischievous to lost in her own pleasure. With her body stretching and molding to him, her thighs tight around his hips, he couldn't have taken it slow if he'd wanted to. Instead he let the force of his desire take over as he thrust into her over and over.

With her breasts bouncing, inviting him to get closer, he lowered himself and pinned her hands over her head. "Do you think you deserve to come tonight?"

His hips stilled with his cock buried deep inside her. She squirmed and moaned. "Please," she whispered.

"You're not such a rebel now that you want something, is that it?"

She strained against his grasp, and he let her go, but only so he could continue, faster and harder, until he could tell by her shallow, quick breathing that she was about to come.

And then he stopped, just as she'd stopped him earlier.

It took all his willpower, and when she squirmed beneath him, tightened her inner muscles around him, he almost lost his last shred of control.

Before he could change his mind, he withdrew.

"Damn you," she whispered, but her eyes revealed the fact that she was enjoying their game.

Resting on one elbow, he slid his fingers inside her and watched her squirm. Then he dipped his head between her legs and buried his face there. He tasted her, licked her, teased her, drank her in. She was so hot and sweet and wet and delicious, like his favorite dish spread out before him in never-ending supply.

With his fingers pumping inside her, he found her

clit with his tongue and worked her toward the climax she was moaning for. It only took moments, and then she was there. Bucking against him, crying out.

Mason sighed against her, wishing for something he couldn't quite name. And then he was on top of her again, buried within her, crashing into her until his own orgasm was coming on strong.

She locked her legs around his hips and held tight to him and he came closer, closer, and then he was there in the rush of his orgasm. He spilled into her, let himself go.

What if this was their last night together?

The question formed in his mind out of nowhere, and he pushed it aside.

He collapsed beside her and pulled her close, tangled his legs with hers and placed a kiss on her forehead. Out of nowhere, he knew that Claire had become too dear to him, that he'd made a huge mistake in letting her stay at the resort. Instead of working her out of his system, she'd worked herself completely under his skin.

Mason gave himself a mental slap. He was thinking crazy—totally understandable given what they'd been doing minutes ago. He just needed to let go, let Claire leave, and in another day or two maybe there'd be another woman to distract him.

He'd forget all about Claire.

"You look like you're in deep thought."

"Just wondering if you're cured yet," he lied.

She sighed, her eyes closed, her expression one of utter relaxation. "Ask me again in ten minutes."

Mason brushed a tendril of hair away from her cheek. With any luck, curing Claire would take the rest of the night.

CLAIRE ABSOLUTELY was not cured.

Not even a little bit.

This, she'd realized, was an enormous problem. As Mason had had his face buried between her legs, his tongue working unspeakable magic, she'd had the horrible realization that her entire trip to Escapade had been a waste.

They'd just finished making love again after having ordered room service for dinner and were lying tangled together on the bed, where Claire couldn't imagine leaving. She wanted to stay all night, all morning, all afternoon....

Even worse, she'd been overcome with emotion where Mason was concerned.

Messy, complicated, wild, uncontrollable emotion. And she didn't dare name it for fear it wouldn't go away if she did.

But then, how could she not name it?

Love.

There it was. That emotion she'd gone to great lengths to avoid in recent years. That girlish, giddy rush that she absolutely did not want to have.

She'd accidentally fallen in love with Mason—or

had she? Was it really possible to love someone she
didn't want to love? Was it possible to take less than
a week of great sex and some good conversation and
turn that into a truly meaningful relationship?

Maybe not. Maybe she'd just let the constant af-
terglow of sex cloud her thinking. Maybe the giddy
emotion she was feeling wasn't love so much as it
was the joy of being well-pleasured. Now *that* was a
joy she hadn't been experiencing lately.

*Not with all her fantasies about Mason preoccu-
pying her and driving her nearly insane.*

Claire's eyes shot open in the darkness as the truth
came to her. She stared at the shadows on the ceil-
ing cast by moonlight through the window, and she
understood the truth.

What she'd been feeling wasn't love. It was simply the side effect of having her fantasies fulfilled.

After all, it wasn't very often that happened to a
woman, and it was a heady experience when it did
happen. Surely she'd just gotten a little befuddled by
all the great sex and fantasy-fulfillment going on.

Claire shifted under the weight of Mason's arm,
testing how easily she might be able to slip out of bed
undetected. In her limited experience, he seemed to
be a pretty heavy sleeper, so she could probably make
a clean break.

She'd promised tonight would be their last night
together, and he clearly wanted her off his island
sooner rather than later. If she could leave now and

avoid any awkward goodbyes, he'd probably be thankful in the morning.

What to do with the fact that she was nowhere near being cured of Mason, she had no idea.

Maybe distance would give her some perspective.... Although a week ago they'd had an entire continent between them and it hadn't done much in the way of giving her perspective.

Quite the opposite, actually.

She'd thought proximity—extreme proximity— would be the cure, and yet here she was as proximate as she could be and completely uncured.

Proximity had not only proven her fantasies correct but had shown her Mason wasn't nearly as annoying once she got to know him a little.

The only thing that hadn't changed from her very first encounter with Mason was the spark in their relationship, both in and out of bed—a spark that could ignite a firestorm if handled improperly.

If handled improperly...

Did the answer to her dilemma lie in the very spark between them? Could it be that she could rid herself of her out-of-control desire for Mason by simply tossing the right kind of kindling into their fire?

They'd had their share of arguments, but recent ones had been mostly in fun, fueled by their mutual love of debate. Perhaps the problem was that Claire had been holding back, being too much of a nice girl to get what she wanted—namely, to be in bed with Mason.

Now that she wanted out of his bed, maybe she just needed to be more herself. Or maybe a slightly exaggerated version of herself...

She'd driven away her share of men, a few of them purely by accident, just by being herself. Men were unusually intimidated by women who were too out-spoken, too strong, too independent. She wasn't the kind of girl a guy could imagine himself protecting from the beasts with his club. She was the kind of girl who'd pick up a club and help chase the beasts away.

And that's just what she needed to do now.

She couldn't deal with another guy walking out on her for not being sweet enough, or compliant enough, or boring enough.

She squirmed and tried to get up, untangling her legs from Mason's and pushing his arm off of her waist, doing her best to wake him up in the process.

He stirred, emitting a low moan, and she nudged his leg with her foot until his eyes opened.

"Hey," he said smiling, his voice gravelly.

"I'm getting out of here."

"I thought you'd stick around for breakfast, at least."

"Sorry, I think we've both gotten what we wanted out of this relationship, wouldn't you say?"

She tried to stand up, but he caught her wrist.

"Did I do something wrong?" he asked.

"No, of course not."

"Then why the rush to leave?"

"I told you I'd get out of your hair once I'd had enough of you."

"So it worked this time?"

"Definitely," she lied.

He pushed himself up in bed and regarded her seriously. "Well then, I guess this is goodbye."

"Don't sound so sad. This is what you want, remember?"

"Don't assume you know what I want."

His words stung for reasons Claire couldn't quite imagine. She needed to make this a smooth, easy break, so that neither of them would have regrets.

Not that Mason would, anyway, but still...

"Listen, thanks for the laughs and all, but don't bother keeping in touch. I'll leave the resort on the next flight I can get out of here."

"No need to rush. Stick around a while longer if you want. Don't leave on account of being cured of me."

Claire wriggled out of his grasp and stood, then started dressing in the ridiculous showgirl costume, the only thing she had to wear. "No offense, but this isn't exactly my idea of a perfect vacation, being trapped here on your crappy little island."

She'd said it just to get an argument started, to ensure their clean break.

"Where's that coming from? Are you trying to start a fight with me?"

For the first time since they'd met, they were actually having trouble arguing.

Amazing.

"Mason, I just don't want us having any regrets after I leave. I know the score with you. I know you don't want a long-term thing, and neither do I."

He slid over to her side of the bed and tried to pull her closer. She stepped away.

"You sure about that?" he asked.

"Don't let your giant ego get in the way, Mason. You just can't stand the thought of a woman walking out on you, is that it?"

"My giant ego? Is this some kind of joke?"

She'd insulted his ego, and he still wasn't getting pissed. This was a lot harder than she'd thought it would be.

"No joke, Mason. You have to know I've never liked you. Not from the first time we met in Arizona. I thought you were an overbearing, controlling bore of a man," she lied.

His eyebrows shot up.

"And I'm glad I stole your Porsche and left you in the desert."

It wasn't true at all. The car "theft" had been a stupid, impulsive decision she'd regretted for months, and she'd been wildly attracted to Mason on their first date.

Back then she'd thought that it was too bad he was such an asshole, and she'd been seriously disturbed that he was the first man she'd ever had such a strong animal reaction to.

Claire distinctly remembered how off-kilter and upset she'd been after her first encounter with Mason. She'd eaten fudge-brownie sundaes for days and had had to spend countless hours at the gym atoning for her dietary transgressions.

No doubt, they were two people who were never meant to be, who probably should have never even met.

"Well, I'm surprised you feel that way," he said, still not as pissed as she'd hoped he would be.

"And for the record, Mason. You've got a small penis."

That was the lie of the century.

He laughed.

"I'm not joking."

His gaze turned incredulous in the shadowy room. "Oh yeah? Well, you hog the covers, and you snore like a truck driver."

"I do not!"

"Is that even your real hair color?" he asked, and Claire knew she'd finally succeeded.

"Screw you." She turned and started to leave.

He followed. "I already did, too many times. And you're right, I don't want a serious relationship with a woman like you."

A woman like her? What the hell did that mean? She was afraid to ask.

Because she knew.

He didn't want a woman as strong as her, as outspoken, as bristly and unapologetic. He wanted a sweet little thing who'd affirm all his opinions and tell him what a great guy he was.

That's what every guy wanted.

The opposite of Claire.

She turned as she was about to walk out the door. "I'm glad we've got that settled then. Don't call me, and I won't call you."

She stepped out and slammed the door, her stomach clenching as she did it.

Okay, this was how she'd wanted it to end, right? With a good, nasty fight?

Now they could part ways with no regrets, no glancing back over shoulders and wondering what might have been?

Yes, that was what she wanted.

Then why did it feel like the most awful thing she'd ever done?

She wandered back to her room feeling a sense of loss but going on autopilot. Somehow she made it there without getting lost, as her thoughts dwelled on Mason.

He'd felt so good to her at times, so perfect, so right. He'd been better than she could have imagined. He'd been her fantasies come to life.

And knowing for sure now that fantasies were just that—something that never panned out in real life—felt like a crushing blow at the moment, like a reason to fall on the floor and cry.

But she'd known all along, hadn't she? Hadn't

she always known that fantasies weren't real? Hadn't that been why she'd come here in the first place?

Of course. Yet having her fantasies dashed so thoroughly was far from her idea of the perfect way to end a vacation.

14

MASON HEARD A KNOCK on his door and immediately thought of Claire. She'd come back.

But why?

Had she changed her mind? Decided to stay another night? Come back to apologize?

None of it sounded likely, but his heart raced as he walked toward the door. In his head he rehearsed his reaction when he opened the door and saw her.

Oh, hi. What's up?

Or…

Did you forget something?

Or… A glimpse through the peephole settled the matter. It was just Carter.

Mason opened the door, feeling crestfallen for reasons he didn't care to examine. "Hey, Carter."

"Hey. Can I come in?"

Mason stepped aside and motioned him in, suddenly feeling too weary to talk.

"I hope I'm not interrupting anything."

"Not at all. What's going on?"

"Just thought I'd stop by and fill you in on what I've found out about the girls who were working for Mike D'Amato."

Business problems were the furthest thing from his mind, but maybe they were the distraction he needed. "Okay, shoot." He motioned for Carter to have a seat on the sofa, and he took a seat in the chair across from him.

"Looks like there are probably four girls involved, all reporting directly to Mike. Since you removed him, the business has come to a halt."

"Where'd you get this information?"

Carter flashed a sheepish grin. "Pillow talk, man. I can't reveal my source, but she's a friend of one of the girls. I gave her a go in bed, and she gave me the info I need. I've got names."

"Turn them over to resort security, and thanks for your help," Mason said, too tired to point out that he didn't agree with Carter's investigative methods.

Carter crossed his arms over his chest and gave Mason a speculative look. "What happened with you and the redhead?"

"Claire? Why do you ask?"

"Just curious. I saw her in the lobby a little while ago looking upset. When I asked her how you and she were doing, she said you were finished."

"How can we be finished when we never got started?"

Carter shrugged. "So there's nothing between you two?"

"Not a thing," Mason lied.

Why he felt compelled to lie, he didn't know. He wasn't even sure he'd told an actual lie…more like a shade of the truth.

"Then you wouldn't mind if I asked her out?"

His question hit Mason like a punch in the gut.

Hell yeah, he'd mind.

But he shouldn't. If he wanted there to be nothing between himself and Claire, then one sure way to make it happen was to give Carter his blessing.

"I think she's planning on leaving, but if you can track her down before she goes, be my guest. Don't say I didn't warn you though—she's nothing but trouble."

Carter smiled. "Looks like a pretty hot kind of trouble to me."

Mason shrugged. "Whatever man. Just watch out."

He resisted the urge to say any more. Part of him wanted to list all of Claire's flaws, make her sound like more hassle than she was worth, when he knew his motive wasn't to protect his friend so much as it was to keep another man away from Claire.

"You sure about this?"

"Absolutely," Mason said and forced a smile.

"All right, then. I'd better go, I've got some work to take care of."

Carter left, leaving Mason standing in the middle of his living room feeling like an ass. What did he care if Carter and Claire hit it off? It wasn't any of his business now, was it?

No, it wasn't.

What he needed was a distraction from Claire.

He stalked over to his desk and flipped open his laptop, then sat down and tried to read the latest headline news on the Internet. But it was all gibberish.

Damn it, Judd was right, he had to get off this island soon. Maybe take a trip to the Fantasy Ranch and oversee its operation for a while, make sure all was running smoothly there. But the thought of being in the same state as Claire unsettled him.

Maybe what he needed was a real vacation, something he hadn't bothered with in years. He'd always wanted to see Paris, Rome, Vienna—this could be his chance to do a great-cities-of-Europe tour. Except the thought of doing it alone didn't thrill him.

He closed his laptop again and stalked over to the patio doors and opened them. A tropical breeze rustled his hair, but for the first time he could remember, he wanted to be anywhere but on his island, at his dream resort.

He should have known Claire Elliot would ruin it all for him sooner or later.

CLAIRE KNOCKED on the door of Lucy and Judd's suite, her heart thudding morosely in her chest for reasons she didn't want to examine.

Lucy opened the door. "Hey, come on in."

Claire nodded to her suitcase. "I'm just stopping to say bye and ask if I can leave my luggage in your room for a little while."

"Bye? You're leaving?"

Claire came inside, dragging her suitcase behind her. "Yeah, long story."

"Of course you can leave your bags here, but what's going on?" She was wearing her worried-friend look now, the one that always assured Claire she had one person in the world who would truly look out for her, no matter what.

"I've just had enough of Mason, that's all. Where's Judd?" She glanced around, not wanting to get into a discussion of Mason's many shortcomings with his brother around.

"He went out to find a newspaper and some portable lunch we can eat here in the room."

"Oh, sorry, am I interrupting your romantic day alone together?" She noticed Lucy's outfit for the first time, a crocheted string-bikini top and a pair of short cutoff jean shorts that left little to the imagination, definitely not Lucy's usual conservative style.

"Not at all." She caught Claire staring. "Oh, this outfit? I thought I'd go a little wild, for old times' sake."

Claire smiled at the memory of Lucy's week of being wild at the Fantasy Ranch. "Wild suits you well, my dear."

"Now tell me what's going on? Why the sudden departure?"

"Like I said—"

"No, I want the whole story. Not your vague excuses."

"I know you had high hopes for Mason and me, but it's just not going to happen. Neither of us want a relationship."

Lucy looked unconvinced. "You really expect me to buy that? Do you have any idea what makes you happy?"

Claire took a step back, surprised by her friend's tone. "Of course I do. Not having jerk-offs in my life makes me happy."

"Do you realize that I've seen you smiling more in the past few days than I have in the past six months?"

Was that true? It couldn't be.

"It's just being on vacation," she explained. "I needed the break."

"Right, even though you went to Bermuda three months ago?"

"That was a work trip."

"Claire, don't you think you might be smiling so much because you've been with a guy who makes you happy?"

"He makes me crazy! That's a lot different than happy."

"I think you like crazy. I think you're happiest when you have someone in your life who challenges you."

Sort of like Lucy did…. The two were so different, it was a wonder to outsiders that they were so close, but it made perfect sense to Claire. She loved debating with Lucy, loved her friend's different point of view that stretched her and made her think about what she believed.

But Mason was nothing like that. "Mason doesn't challenge me. He makes me want to punch holes in walls."

"You say that, but I haven't seen you punching anything. What I've seen is you happy, relaxed, having the time of your life."

"Let's just agree to disagree, okay?"

"Claire, you're always dating guys who are totally wrong for you because you know you won't get hurt that way."

"That's ridiculous," Claire said, a sick feeling settling in her belly.

"I just want you to take a risk in your personal life so that you can be happy."

"I am happy!"

Was she? Aside from the uncontrollable fantasies, sure she was.

But... Well, okay. She had felt happier this week at the resort than she had in a long time, but really it had to have been the beautiful setting and the great sex. What girl wouldn't be happy with that?

"Did you ever stop to think that maybe you're not supposed to boss your boyfriends around and expect them to behave like your hired servants?"

"I don't do that."

"Claire, you absolutely do! You treat guys like dirt knowing they'll either walk away or stick around for a while until you get bored with them because they're not a challenge for you. And then you're free to move on without getting hurt. That's your MO."

MO? Ever since she'd married a private investigator, Lucy's language had become peppered with stuff like that.

"I didn't realize I had an MO," Claire said, half wanting to protest and half accepting that Lucy was right.

"I'm sorry if I sound a little harsh. I just want to see you as happy as you've been this week all the time."

"It can't be with Mason, Luc. He's wanted me to leave ever since I got here, and I'm overwhelmed with relief to finally be going."

"Because you're afraid."

"Okay, maybe in the past I've made some rather shallow choices in men. Maybe I've deliberately chosen guys I knew I wouldn't get attached to, but this time, I'm walking away from a guy I can't get attached to."

Lucy's jaw was set. She'd decided long ago that Mason was the guy for Claire, and no amount of proof was going to change her normally levelheaded friend's mind.

"Face it, Luc. Even you have to be wrong every once in a while."

"Have you at least let Mason know you're leaving and given him a chance to stop you?"

"Absolutely. I told him late last night, and he certainly didn't beg me to stay."

Lucy sighed. "You two drive me crazy."

"That's my job," Claire said with a little smile she didn't really feel.

Lucy hugged Claire and then smiled. "I hope you have a safe trip home. I'll see you back there next week, okay?"

"Have fun with that husband of yours. I'm off to grab a drink while I wait for my flight this evening. I leave at five."

They said their goodbyes, and Claire told Lucy she'd be back around four to get her bag. She wandered outside, her thoughts confused after having talked to Lucy.

Had she really been sabotaging her love life? Claire would be the first to admit she didn't like long-term relationships. She wasn't interested in getting too cozy with any one guy. After all, life was short, and she wanted to see and do it all. She couldn't very well do that if she settled down.

And besides, she had a plan. When she was thirty-five, she'd settle down a little bit and let herself be more open to the idea of a permanent guy in her life. Until then though, she was a free agent, and she liked it that way.

Claire made her way to the Cabana Club, where she knew she could get an unequaled martini. She found a seat at the bar and placed her order, then glanced around to see who else was present. The resort's entertainment director, Carter somebody-or-other, was standing at the end of the bar, and when he saw her, he smiled and headed toward her.

She'd bumped into him in the lobby earlier and thought he was cute, though she didn't usually go for blondes.

"Hey, I've been looking all over for you," he said, sitting down beside her.

"For *me?*"

His smile grew playful. "Yeah, you. I noticed you the first time I saw you here."

Claire sipped her drink and smiled. "I see. And why were you just looking for me?"

Carter was clearly into his own looks. His sun-streaked hair was styled just so, and his perfectly tanned skin and sculpted muscles looked more acquired by tanning beds and weightlifting than hours spent outdoors on a sports field.

"A little bird told me you and Mason are no longer an item, and I was wondering if you'd like to have dinner."

"Actually, I'm flying back to Arizona tonight."

"I was hoping to convince you not to. I noticed your reservation actually goes through Sunday."

Claire blinked. This was certainly an interesting turn of events. There might not be any better way to forget a guy than to have some fun with another one....

"I really should go. Mason's not going to be happy if I stick around."

Carter waved away her statement. "Don't worry about him. I already talked to him and told him I wanted to ask you out. He gave his blessing, if it makes any difference to you."

Claire blinked, trying not to look offended. "It's really not his place to be giving blessings on who I do or don't go out with."

"Does that mean you'll have dinner with me?"

His offer was tempting.

She smiled. "I don't know. Let me think about it, and I'll get back to you in a little while. I'd have to make some arrangements, change my flights around again…."

"Sure," he said. "How about we get a table and have a drink while you're thinking about it?"

The man was nothing if not persistent. She hated drinking alone, so she nodded. "Okay, one drink."

With any luck, Mason would wander into the bar and spot them together. If he wanted to sleep alone for the rest of his life, if he was willing to let her walk away without a protest, all the better for her. But Claire didn't see any reason why she couldn't make sure he knew that even if he didn't want her, there were plenty of guys who did.

Even guys he knew and considered his friends.

Okay, so maybe she was being petty, but she'd nearly allowed herself to fall in love with Mason, and all she'd gotten in return was his company in bed. A pretty good prize, but still. She didn't dare give her heart to just anyone.

Carter stood and waited for her to do the same, then slipped his hand under her arm and led her to a secluded table in the corner.

They sat down across from each other, and Claire willed herself to act interested. She should have felt happy to be having a drink with Carter, but something about him just felt a little…off.

Whatever it was, she couldn't put her finger on it. Or maybe she was just being overly critical to keep her distance from any new guys right now.

"You look like you've got something on your mind," he said.

"Me? Just thinking I'd like another martini."

He smiled. "Coming right up."

Carter caught the attention of a waitress and motioned her over, then placed Claire's drink order and asked for a refill of his own drink, too.

Claire realized it had been all day since she'd touched up her makeup, and she began to wonder if the spinach tart she'd had for lunch was lingering anywhere on her teeth. She smiled at Carter and stood up.

"I need to use the ladies' room. I'll be right back."

Claire went to the restroom and studied herself in the mirror, relieved to find no traces of spinach. She dug around in her bag until she found her lipstick, then applied a fresh coat, mussed up her hair a bit, and decided that would have to be good enough for Carter.

Her heart didn't feel in this at all. She could barely care what Carter thought of her, appearance or otherwise. But he was a hot guy, close enough to her type under normal circumstances, as far as she could tell. Sure, there had seemed like something was off about him, something that had her a little on edge, but maybe it was just her impending ride on a propeller plane back to Miami that had her feeling edgy.

Yes, that was probably it.

She returned to the table and found Carter talking on his cell phone. When he saw her, he wrapped up the call immediately, snapped his phone shut and tucked it into his pocket.

"Hey lady," he said, flashing a playboy smile.

Claire sat down and took a sip of her martini.

Carter watched her. "Hard to believe Mason let a catch like you get away."

Claire shrugged. "It was a mutual thing. Neither of us were looking for love."

"Ah. You're just a tigress on the prowl then, eh?"

Carter was turning out to be a little annoying. Claire glanced around the bar, wondering how long she'd have to endure this conversation.

"I guess you could say that," she said, forcing a smile at him.

She sipped her drink, but it left an odd aftertaste.

She glanced down at it and frowned. "This is a crappy martini," she said.

"Want me to order you something different? Maybe a Screaming Orgasm?"

Oh yeah, Carter was a real class act. Claire glanced at her watch and wondered if he knew the flight schedules well enough to know she was lying if she said her flight was about to leave.

But her thoughts started feeling like they were moving through mud, and she was having trouble thinking of the words to form a sentence. What was it she wanted to say, anyway?

Claire wasn't a lush, but she could usually hold a martini without getting tipsy. Hadn't she eaten enough for lunch? Why was she feeling like she was sixteen and had just downed her first shot of whiskey?

"Hey, I was thinking, maybe we could take a little walk on the beach after this—what do you say?"

Hmm, what did she say? Why wasn't her mouth working? Claire closed her eyes and tried to steady herself, but suddenly she was feeling very, very tipsy.

Yeah, maybe some sea air would do her good.

"Um, sure," she finally managed to say. "I must not have eaten enough for lunch.... I think this drink has gone to my head a bit."

Carter placed some bills on the table. "Come on," he said. "I'll carry you if you're too tipsy to walk."

Claire let him take her hand and lead her out of the bar, feeling a vague sense of disappointment that

Mason hadn't shown up, but now she couldn't quite remember why she'd wanted him there, anyway.

They left the center of the resort and headed for the ocean, with Claire stumbling along the way. Carter had to hold her up to keep her from falling once, then again. Guests and various landmarks they must have been passing looked more like blurs to her, and it took all her mental energy to focus on putting one foot in front of the other.

A fleeting thought came to her: odd that Carter seemed to be taking them away from the populated section of beach, toward the rocky beaches that bordered the jungle.

But she couldn't quite summon the words to question their direction, and so she followed along, stumbling in her sandals until she finally thought to just take them off.

Carter was talking to her now, but she wasn't registering the words. Wha-wha-whawha-wha, wha-whawha…

Huh?

He turned and looked at her. "Claire? Do you hear me?"

She meant to nod yes, but instead she mumbled, "I need to sit." And she promptly sat down on the sand, unable to walk another step with her head spinning and her body feeling so out of her control.

"Here's as good a place as any," he said, sitting down beside her.

Claire got an odd feeling. Something definitely wasn't right.

Carter leaned forward, his lips only inches from hers now. "I'll bet you're a really hot lay," he said, his breath smelling of beer. "You ever screw in the jungle?"

Oh God. This was going very, very wrong. Claire struggled to stand up, but her body wasn't moving.

"Don't bother," Carter said, reaching out and grasping her breast, his touch rough and invasive. He squeezed her and pressed her breast upward. "In a few minutes you'll be passed out."

"What?"

"Are you really that dumb? You think you just had a bad martini, you stupid little bitch?"

Oh God, oh God, oh God. Claire was paralyzed with fear for the first time in her life, sure she was in deep trouble and completely unable to help herself.

Again she struggled to stand up, but her body had turned to lead, and everything around her was getting hazy.

Carter pushed her down into the sand and climbed on top of her. Claire tried to scream, but all she heard was a pitiful yelp before his hand covered her mouth. "Too bad you're gonna be asleep for the screw of your life," he said, grinding his hips into her.

And then she heard voices she didn't recognize. The sounds of laughter and talking. Carter covered her mouth with a rough kiss and didn't let up.

Someone was beside them now, but Claire couldn't look over. She felt herself beginning to black out as a strange voice said, "Oh, sorry guys, we thought we were alone here. Hope you don't mind if we spread out our beach towels over there."

15

MASON COULD HARDLY believe what he'd heard. A waitress from one of the bars had come to him, teary-eyed, and confessed that she knew Carter Cayhill was behind some nefarious goings-on at the resort.

What had at first sounded unbelievable quickly settled in Mason's head as truth. Carter, his friend and his sounding board, had betrayed him in the worst kind of way. It made terrible sense.

The waitress had been afraid to come forward for fear of losing her job, but when she'd seen him disappear from the bar with Mason's "girlfriend," the two of them looking suspicious, she'd felt compelled to finally come forward.

She said she'd heard rumors of him running a prostitution ring there at the resort, and she'd seen a few suspicious transactions happen between him and the bartenders on more than one occasion.

Mason hadn't waited to hear any more. He wanted to find Carter and Claire before anything happened between them so that he could be sure

Claire knew what kind of guy she was dealing with.
Why that was so important to him, he didn't want
to examine.

The waitress had said she'd had a bad vibe about
Carter's intentions with Claire, and Mason had to
trust that. Who knew what the man was capable of if
he'd been behind the prostitution ring.

She'd said she had seen them heading toward the
north beach, and Mason had set off on foot, using his
radio to contact security and alert them to the possible situation and to start a search for Carter.

Mason's walk turned to a run as he neared the
edge of the main entrance area. He knew a spot in the
jungle where Carter had once bragged about taking
a woman. It was a shot in the dark searching there
first, but it was also all he had to go on.

Fueled by anger and a growing sense of betrayal,
Mason raced across the resort, the fact of Carter's in-
volvement in the prostitution ring pounding in his
head. How could Carter have lied so blatantly? How
could he have pretended to be a friend? How could
Mason have been so damn gullible? He didn't have
any answers, just the growing urge to punch something or someone.

Fifteen minutes later, he was wandering the edge
of the jungle, following footpaths worn by hiking
tourists and feeling an animal sort of fury now. He
saw a couple having a picnic, sitting on towels spread
out on the sand, and he approached them.

"Excuse me, but did you see a man and a woman here a little while ago? He's blond, she's a red-head—"

They peered up at him, squinting in the summer sun. "Oh right," the woman said. "They went off into the jungle. I think we sort of interrupted them."

"Thanks," Mason said as he headed toward the edge of the woods.

A minute later, when he spotted a white sandal lying in the brush and recognized it as Claire's, his every sense went on alert, fear mingling with his fury. A missing shoe couldn't be a good sign.

If anything happened to Claire…

Anything at all, and he'd kill Carter.

Where had this rush of emotion come from? Why was he feeling so damn possessive of a woman he'd been sure he wanted to be rid of only hours ago?

Because Claire turned him into a fool.

And because he wanted her.

The realization nearly stopped him in his tracks. Why hadn't he seen it sooner? Probably because he hadn't been looking for it, hadn't been looking for a relationship, and definitely hadn't been expecting to like Claire as much as he did.

He wanted her.

But what was the likelihood she'd want him, too?

Virtually none, since she'd been the one about to hurry off the island in the first place.

Mason peered into the jungle, banishing the self-ish thoughts from his head. He had to focus on finding Claire, regardless of anything else.

And then he heard the telltale sound of plants rustling, and he froze, his every sense on alert.

He edged closer to where the sound had come from, silently pushing aside plants as his gaze scanned every gap in the greenery.

Maybe he'd just heard birds rustling around in the leaves, or maybe Claire was nearby, in trouble.

He searched for what felt like hours but couldn't have been more than minutes, and finally he saw them.

Claire lay lifeless on the ground, twenty feet away, in a secluded spot where he never would have seen them if he hadn't been looking closely. Sunlight danced on the darkened jungle floor, creating odd patterns and flashes of light, temporarily blinding Mason. When he was able to focus again, he saw Carter kneeling down, unfastening his belt.

Mason sprung into motion, his feet pounding the jungle floor as he closed the distance between them. "Carter Cayhill, damn it! You bastard."

Carter looked up and spotted him just as he was pulling Claire's dress up.

A lump of rage rose up in Mason's chest, and he wanted to pummel Carter for daring to touch her.

But she wasn't his.

Didn't want to be his.

"What the hell?" Carter said, standing up and adjusting his pants.

"I know you're behind the prostitution ring, Carter. Security is on its way here now," Mason lied, "so you'd better come with me."

He looked down at Claire, who he realized now was lying lifeless on the ground.

"She had a little too much to drink, man. She's out."

"You son of a bitch, what did you do to her?"

Mason pushed Carter out of the way, then dropped to his knees beside Claire and felt for her pulse.

But then something hard made contact with his jaw, and he went flying backwards, landing on his back in the brush. His cheek was throbbing, and Carter sprung onto him, grabbing his throat and squeezing his airway shut.

Mason struggled and bucked against the assault, finally breaking free of Carter's hold and toppling him, buying himself time to grab a nearby rock and wield it near Carter's temple.

"One wrong move and I'll knock you out, too."

He needed to radio security, before things got any more out of hand. But then he heard the familiar squawk of a walkie-talkie, and he breathed a sigh of relief. Security had found them.

"Over here!" he yelled.

A few moments later, two security guards appeared. They dragged Carter up from the ground, then handcuffed him as he struggled and cursed.

"We'll take him back to admin, sir," one of the guards said.

"Radio medical right away," Mason said, nodding at Claire. "I think she's been drugged."

The second guard called back to have emergency medical come right away and roughly described their location.

"You brought this on yourself, Mason. You and your cocky attitude, thinking you can tell me how to do my job, thinking you know every damn thing about running a resort. You should have listened to my ideas every once in a while, asshole."

His ideas?

Oh, right, his ideas. Right around the time Escapade opened, Carter had come to Mason spouting some pretty lousy ideas about how to improve the entertainment side of the business, and Mason had laughed, had even thought he was joking.

So this is what Carter does in return? "You're a real piece of work. I thought you were my friend."

Carter laughed as the security guards began leading him back toward the resort. "Yeah, I figured being your buddy was the best way to stay out from under your scrutiny."

So that he could operate his prostitution ring undetected.

Of course. It all made sickening sense now, and he'd been a fool to trust Carter.

He went to Claire's side and dropped to his knees

beside her, suddenly more terrified than he'd ever been in his life. When he looked at her, so frail and lifeless, his chest contracted and the air disappeared from his lungs.

If anything happened to her, he'd have himself to blame. No one but himself.

He'd been a fool in more ways than one.

MASON FORCED HIS LUNGS to work. Air in. Air out. He took a deep breath, forcing his tight chest to expand as far as it would go.

Claire was going to be okay.

Doctor Collins had just spoken those words so casually, as if Mason's entire world hadn't hinged on hearing them. Yet his body couldn't relax all at once, but rather in small increments with each successive breath.

Claire's face was pale, her body still and limp.

"Has she been drugged?" Mason managed to ask.

Collins nodded. "I'm guessing she's been given a dose of Rohypnol. If so, she'll wake up disoriented and probably won't remember anything that's happened since she was drugged."

Mason was almost too afraid to ask, "Was there any sign of…abuse or mistreatment?"

The doctor shook his head. "None. It's a good thing you found them before anything happened. She might have a few bumps and bruises, but she'll be fine."

Thank God.

"When will she wake up?"

The doctor shrugged. "Depends on when she was given the drug and how big a dose she consumed."

"That's the best you can tell me?"

"Her vital signs are good, just a slightly elevated heart rate. I'd guess she could wake up any time now. It's best to let her sleep rather than trying to rouse her."

"I'd like to at least move her somewhere more comfortable," Mason said.

"Of course. We'll use the gurney to move her to my office where she can rest until she wakes up."

Mason glanced over at the gurney and medical attendant he hadn't noticed until now. He'd been so focused on Claire, the rest of the world had faded away.

"I'd like to wait with her," he said, ready to stand his ground if Collins resisted the idea.

"You're a friend?"

How to describe his relationship with Claire... They weren't officially a couple, and yet she felt like far more than his friend. They were former lovers, definitely, but that too seemed a sadly inadequate descriptor. "She's actually my girlfriend," he said finally, settling for the easiest response.

Dr. Collins raised an eyebrow, probably thinking about Mason's reputation. He'd never been one for commitment—that much was true.

"That's fine," he said. "Just keep in mind that

she'll need some time to adjust and wrap her mind around this incident."

"Got it."

Mason followed the doctor and his assistant as they pushed Claire on the gurney along the garden path and across the resort to its small medical clinic. Serious medical problems were cause for airlift to Miami, but most non-critical ailments could be handled there on the island, and Doctor Brian Collins was among the best. Mason felt totally secure trusting Claire in the doctor's care.

But that didn't mean he'd leave her side.

The whorl of emotions in his gut felt like a smaller version of the tropical storm that had skirted the island last weekend. The sounds of the birds in the trees nearby, the warm wind that rustled his hair—it all seemed surreal and out of place when Claire was lying motionless on a gurney.

In the small clinic, Mason sat on a chair next to her and watched her sleep, grateful for the steady rise and fall of her chest. In the silence, he was finally able to relax.

What did all this mean? He couldn't imagine letting Claire walk away from him now, and he couldn't imagine life without her.

The thought should have felt like a bolt of lightning striking him, but in the tense moments when he'd feared for her life, it had worked its way into his subconscious until he could only accept it as truth.

He loved Claire.

He wanted her more than any woman who had come before, and he wanted her for keeps.

In the space of a few hours, his entire life had been turned upside down, and for once, he didn't want to set it straight again. He wanted all the messy emotions, the unpredictability and the craziness that life with Claire promised.

He wanted it more than anything.

And now that he knew what he wanted, knew how he felt, the bad-seafood feeling that had been haunting him disappeared. All of a sudden, he felt completely right. At peace, even.

The only question that remained was whether Claire would want him, too.

When her eyelids finally fluttered open and she looked around at her surroundings, Mason felt the weight of uncertainty settle on his chest, combined with relief that she really was okay. This was a woman who'd been ready to walk away from him for good only hours ago.

She blinked at him and pushed up on her elbows, then sat up completely. "What... What happened?" She took in the room, the gurney, her tattered, stained clothes. "How did I—and you—where's Carter?"

"Long story."

Having stood up the moment her eyes opened, Mason sat down next to her on the gurney. She gave him an odd look, and Mason asked, "What's the last thing you can remember?"

Claire frowned. "I don't know. I feel like I've been sleeping for a year. What are you doing here?"

The hostility in her voice couldn't be mistaken. While Mason had been having his life-changing experience, Claire had been sleeping. For her, nothing had changed between them.

"Carter drugged you and took you into the jungle, but we caught him before anything happened."

She seemed to be searching her memory for any recollection of the events.

"The resort doctor examined you and said you were likely given a dose of Rohypnol, and that you won't be able to remember anything from the time you were drugged. It knocked you out for a couple of hours."

"I remember being with Carter at the bar. We were talking, and... I remember commenting on my drink tasting strange."

Her eyes widened as the truth settled in on her. "He drugged me."

"You're okay though. Nothing happened."

"I was an idiot for trusting him. My instincts told me something was a little off about him."

"You couldn't have known what he would do."

She shook her head. "I left him with my drink while I went to the restroom. I gave him the perfect opportunity to slip something into it. I should know better after hearing all those warnings about date-rape drugs and never leaving your drink unattended at a bar."

"Claire, stop blaming yourself. Carter had everyone fooled, including me. He was the one running the prostitution ring."

Her eyes widened. "Wow. I'm glad you found your culprit."

"I am, too."

She leveled an indecipherable look at him. It wasn't filled with hatred, at least. "Thank you for saving me. I guess I'm just not used to being in a position of needing to be saved."

"Especially not by me, right?"

She stood up from the gurney, still holding on to the edge of it to steady herself.

"You feel okay?"

"Yes," she said, and Mason could hear a familiar coldness in her voice again. "What time is it? Too late for me to catch a flight back to Miami?"

The thought of her leaving twisted his gut into a knot. "There's still one more flight out this evening, but we need to talk first."

"I think we've said everything that needs to be said."

He dared to reach out and cover her hand with his. She glared at his hand, then up at him. "Not everything," he said.

"If seeing me with Carter, or seeing me in danger, or whatever, gave you some misguided notion that you still want me, forget about it."

A slap in the face couldn't have stung any more than her words did. "Claire, I know how you feel about me—or how you think you feel about me—but can you put aside the anger for a few minutes and hear me out?"

"You're presuming to know how I feel, too?"

"You've made it pretty clear. Now I need to be clear about how I feel. I love you," he blurted before she could interrupt him or storm out the door.

Claire opened her mouth as if to speak, but for once he'd managed to leave her speechless. The hostility drained from her expression. "I'm sorry this whole mess has left you so confused, Mason." She withdrew her hand from his. "But there's no way you can mean that."

"I do mean it," he said. "Why don't you stay another week and let me convince you."

"I can't. I need to be back in Phoenix, and besides, I know trouble when I see it now." She offered him a weary smile and edged toward the door. "You and me? We're nothing but trouble together."

Mason felt as if his one true chance at happiness were slipping from his fingers, and the sensation stopped him cold. How had he gotten so crazy? How had he let himself fall in love with Claire?

Stupid question. He'd known from their very first encounter that she was right for him. That's why he'd been sabotaging them from the start. He hadn't wanted to find anyone to fall in love with.

"I'll come to Phoenix then," he said.

She shook her head. "No, don't." Her gaze turned flinty. "I mean it."

And with that she walked out the door. The sound of her footsteps retreating on the hallway tiles left him feeling hollow, empty, alone.

Three words, he realized miserably, that aptly described his entire life without Claire.

16

CLAIRE HATED PROPELLER planes. She may have been a seasoned traveler, but sitting on a tiny aircraft, hearing the noisy whir of the engine, feeling every bump and rattle of turbulence that knocked such a small airplane through the sky, made her wish she could just stay in one place.

The flight attendant closed and sealed the aircraft door, then began going through the routine safety procedures brief. A few passengers paid attention, while others read magazines or shuffled through their bags. Claire tried to force herself to listen to the instructions she'd already heard countless times.

Anything to keep herself from looking out the window at the palm trees swaying in the wind and the sky turning orangey-pink on the horizon. Anything to keep herself from thinking of staying.

Anything to keep from thinking about giving her and Mason another chance.

It would be crazy.

Insane.

A fool's pursuit.

Then why had some little part of her been aching to go back to Mason ever since she'd walked out the door of the clinic?

In case of a water landing, the seat cushion may be used as a flotation device.

To distract herself, Claire imagined having to pry the seat cushion from the seat as the plane filled with water, but that only made her even sicker to her stomach. She wanted the hell off this plane.

And she didn't.

She was just letting her fear of propeller planes get to her. No way did she really want to go running back into Mason's arms. Not after all the time they'd spent proving how wrong they were for each other.

Arguing, fighting, butting heads…

Making love, laughing, talking…

She couldn't let herself romanticize their time together now. She had to keep her memories accurate. Force herself to remember it how it really was.

But when she tried, her thoughts focused on how right she'd felt in Mason's arms, how their bodies had worked so perfectly together, how he'd made her laugh harder than anyone else ever had, how when they'd had those long talks over meals, during walks, and in the early morning hours after making love, she'd felt like she'd found her soul mate.

No.

If she remembered those things, then she also had

to remember the arguments, the frustration, the very obvious fact that they were both too strong-willed to be more than temporary lovers.

And most important, she had to remember that until this evening, Mason hadn't wanted a serious relationship with her. He may have been feeling confused thanks to Carter drugging her this afternoon, but come tomorrow, the danger would fade and Mason would be back to his old playboy ways.

But her father popped into her head then. Her father, who she realized now was a lot like Mason. And Mason was the first guy she'd ever met whom she'd let see the real her, the side of her that only her father and her best friend knew. The side of her susceptible to falling in love with a guy just like Mason.

Mason may have been the only guy she'd ever thought could match the standard set by her father, but she'd been wrong. If Claire gave him another chance, she'd get hurt again.

No doubt.

Except, that is, for the giant lump of doubt that had settled in her belly and was expanding by the second, threatening to rise up into her throat.

Or maybe that was just the fear of propeller planes getting to her, confusing her. Yes, that had to be it.

No.

Yes.

No.

The plane's engine grew louder, and it began rolling forward down the runway, preparing for takeoff.

Claire felt herself reaching for her seat belt, unbuckling it, standing up from her seat.

"Wait!" she heard herself yell.

What the hell was she doing?

The nagging voice of common sense was getting drowned out by the sound of the plane's engines as Claire raced up the aisle. The flight attendant, wearing a stern look, stood up from her seat and scolded her. "Sit down immediately! You have to be in your seat for takeoff."

"I have to get off this plane! It's an emergency."

An emergency sounded a little dramatic, but she could think of no other word to describe the driving force that had propelled her from her seat and down the aisle.

"Ma'am, you'd better be serious about this," the flight attendant said, looking doubtful.

"I am. Please stop the plane."

Other passengers were watching the spectacle and murmuring among themselves. A man seated nearby said, "Hurry up and let her off so we can get to Miami."

"Have a seat and I'll see what I can do," the flight attendant said, then turned and went to the cockpit.

A moment later she returned and nodded at Claire just as the plane slowed to a stop. She unlocked and opened the plane's door again, then lowered the stairs for Claire to exit.

On shaky feet, Claire raced down the rickety steps and out onto the Tarmac, then jogged the distance back to the shuttles, where one was just about to leave for the resort.

Claire sat among passengers looking weary from long flights, some of whom must have witnessed her hasty exit from the plane judging by their curious stares. She avoided eye contact and tried to get the jumble of thoughts straight in her head.

What the hell was she doing?

She was afraid of the answer, but she knew. She needed to see Mason one more time. She needed to know, once and for all, if he really and truly loved her.

She needed to find out if they had a chance together. And then what?

Would she be ready to commit? Would she be ready to take the biggest chance of her life?

She wouldn't know the answer until she saw him.

When the shuttle bus stopped in front of the resort's main entrance, Claire exited and raced into the lobby to the reception desk. Skirting the line of guests, she caught the eye of an employee and gave the woman a pleading look.

"Mason Walker—where is he?" she asked.

The woman must have recognized her as Mason's recent companion because she came to the counter and smiled. "He's not in his office, but he was here a few minutes ago. I heard him say he was going for a walk."

"A walk?"

The woman, whose name tag read Celeste, nodded. "If I had to guess, I'd say he's probably on the south beach. He goes there sometimes."

Claire smiled. "Thanks, Celeste."

Celeste smiled back. "Good luck. We all think you two belong together."

We all? Claire felt her cheeks warm at the thought that she and Mason were the source of gossip among the resort employees. But whatever.

She waved and took off for the beach.

Twenty minutes later, her feet were coated with sand, her hair had been whipped into a ratty mess by the wind, and Mason was nowhere in sight. She was about to give up her beachcombing when she spotted a lone figure down the beach, perched on a large piece of driftwood, watching the sunset.

Mason.

A crazy-giddy-nervous feeling stopped her in her tracks, and she felt like she might lose her lunch.

This was it. Her last chance to run away or confront Mason and decide their fate.

Together or apart.

Which would it be?

Then he turned and saw her. He rose up and came walking toward her, and Claire willed her feet to move. Forward, backward, somewhere. But she couldn't move.

Now he was close enough that she could see his

puzzled expression, feel his gaze searching her for answers.

"Hi," he called out, managing to make it a sort of question.

Claire whispered, "Hello," knowing he couldn't hear her, but suddenly unable to make her voice work.

Now he was a few feet away.... A foot... A matter of inches.

The breath whooshed from Claire's lungs.

"What happened to your flight?" he asked.

"I made the plane stop during takeoff. I got off."

"Why?"

"I had to see you."

His expression went from searching to surprised and back again. Nearby, a seagull cried and a large wave crashed near the beach, sending the water racing toward them. Claire felt it engulf her feet up to her ankles, but she couldn't look away from Mason.

"Here I am," he said.

"Here you are."

"Now what?"

"I think we should probably kiss."

Mason reached out and circled her hips with his hands, then pulled her to him. He kissed her slowly, tentatively, like a man who didn't know where he stood.

She felt like she'd come home.

Far away from her condo in Phoenix, far away from her job, her life, everything she knew, on the beach with a man who'd turned her world on its head, she was finally home.

He broke the kiss. "Now what?"

"I don't know," she whispered.

"Do you love me?" he asked.

She surprised herself by answering without hesitation. "Yes."

"I love you, too," Mason said, and she melted into him.

Claire hadn't realized how much she'd ached to hear those words again and how sweet they'd sound when she finally heard them.

He continued. "Sounds like we need to do something about this."

Claire nodded, her throat constricted by a wave of unexpected emotion.

"We can't keep butting heads if we're in love, can we?"

A laugh erupted from her throat, clearing the way for speech. "Actually, I think we can."

"But we shouldn't."

"No, we should try to get along."

"We were doing a pretty good job of it for a while there," he said, smiling.

"I think we can do it again."

"Our entire lives?" he asked.

Claire's jaw dropped, and he smiled that sexy smile of his that could make women strip naked.

"Will you marry me, Claire?"

Her eyes burned with tears, but she didn't have to think over his offer. It might have been unexpected, but she suddenly knew it was the question she'd wanted most to hear.

"Are you sure about this?" she asked.

Mason, perpetual bachelor, the guy who'd eluded marriage in spite of his famous eligibility, couldn't possibly have understood what he was saying.

"I've never been so sure about anything, so no more questions from you." He hugged her tighter against him, mischief dancing in his eyes. "I want an answer."

For once, she was obliged to heed his demand. And as crazy as it seemed even to her, she knew there was only one answer. "Yes, I will."

"We'd better do it fast then, before you change your mind."

"I'm not going to change my mind!" But she had no objections to a fast marriage. She'd always believed in going for what she wanted sooner rather than later.

"And I have every intention of pulling out all the stops to keep you satisfied."

He placed a soft kiss on her lips that grew into a hungry one, and Claire smiled inwardly. She loved Mason's idea of satisfaction.

Sweet, hot, all-night satisfaction.

Epilogue

One week later...

MASON BENT AND CUFFED his tuxedo pants for the third
time that day to keep the sand off of them, smirking
at his bare feet. Not only had he never imagined his
own wedding, he'd definitely never imagined it happening on the beach without shoes. It had been Claire's
idea for them to get married in the exact spot where
he'd proposed to her, and he'd loved it, considering the
secluded beach was his favorite place on the island.

The photographer was busy packing up his equipment, and Lucy and Judd were waiting for them to
all walk together back to the wedding reception.

Claire had other plans.

Claire, his wife. For a guy who'd made a hobby
of avoiding commitment, those three words gave him
inexplicable satisfaction.

No, not inexplicable. Just unexpected.

And if Mason had learned anything in the past few
weeks, it was that the unexpected blessings in life
were the best ones.

"We've got to lose them," Claire whispered, and Mason nodded, trying to keep a straight face.

"Judd, Luc, we'll be back at the reception soon. We'd like to take a walk alone, if you guys don't mind."

"Of course not," Lucy said, but she eyed them suspiciously.

"See you in a few!" Claire called as they walked off.

"I know a secluded spot in this cove up ahead," Mason said as they walked.

Claire smiled. "You know how to hook a girl, that's for sure."

He took her hand and they walked across the sand and along the border of the dense tropical forest that edged the beach, to the cove. In the canopy above, birds sang and chirped, and the sound of the ocean faded a bit.

This was Mason's other favorite spot on the island.

"Do you think we'll be late for our own reception?" Claire asked.

"I don't care if we are. The party can start without us."

"Maybe if we're quick—"

"Not likely," he said, fully intending to take his time and savor their first time making love as husband and wife.

He lifted up the skirt of her dress and found that she was wearing an exquisite little pair of beaded white-lace panties. "Too bad these will have to come off. Hate to get sand on them."

Claire tugged them off and tossed them aside. "No worries."

She unfastened his pants and took him out. She ran her fingers along the ridge of his cock, sending a shudder through him.

Mason lifted her up and rested her weight against the nearest palm tree. With his bride's limbs wrapped around him, her body pressed against him, her breath on his cheek, he felt happier than he ever had in his life.

He slid inside her in one delicious thrust, and when her hot, wet flesh enveloped him, it was the sweetest sensation he'd ever known.

"Thank you," he whispered.

Claire's face was softened with satisfaction, but she gave him a quizzical look. "For this? I think it's called my wifely duty," she said with a wry smile.

"No, for making my life complete."

Claire blinked, and he could see an uncharacteristic dampness in her eyes. "It's the very least I can do," she said, her smile fading as he thrust deeper inside her, filling her completely.

Her face transformed with pleasure, and he knew he'd never tire of seeing her the way she looked right now. Never lose the thrill of holding her, loving her, exploring her.

And the very least he could do was spend the rest of his life making Claire happy. Starting right now, up against the palm tree.

HARLEQUIN® *Blaze*™

Sometimes the biggest mistakes are the best ones....

"I, Denise Cooke, take thee, Redford DeMoss, to be my lawful husband...." No, wait...I did that already—three years ago in a Vegas chapel after one too many Long Island Iced Teas. I married a hunky U.S. Marine I'd met only hours before. (The uniform did it.) The wedding night—week—was spectacular. Then Redford went back to the Gulf. And I went back to my real life as a New York City financial planner...and filed for an annulment.

I'm dating Barry the stockbroker these days, but I think about Redford...a lot. And now, thanks to an upcoming IRS audit, I'm about to see ex-husband again. So why am I flustered? He's probably married, and I have—um, what's his name. It's not as if Redford plans to take me back...or take me—gulp—to bed. Besides, I'd never make the same mistake twice. Not even my favorite one...

#169 MY FAVORITE MISTAKE
by Stephanie Bond

Available in February wherever Harlequin books are sold.

If you enjoyed what you just read,
then we've got an offer you can't resist!

Take 2 bestselling
love stories FREE!
Plus get a FREE surprise gift!